"It's okay, Cody," ... cuddling the bab... "I'm here to take ...

Wilder stepped in front of the door, as if to block her escape, and crossed those strong arms over his impressive chest again. "What are you talking about?" Though he kept his volume low so as not to disturb the sleeping infant, there was no mistaking the steel in his words. "You're not going anywhere with that baby."

"Of course I am," she said. "I'm his aunt. He belongs with me."

"If his mother believed that, why'd she drive halfway across the country to bring him to me?" he challenged.

Beth faltered. "I don't know. But my sister's done a lot of things in her life that I can't begin to fathom."

"Or maybe you do know and you just don't want to tell me," Wilder suggested. "Because it seems obvious to me that there must be a reason Leighton didn't want you caring for her baby."

"*Her* baby?" she echoed. "You don't think he's your baby, too?"

"I don't know what to think," he admitted.

* * *

MONTANA MAVERICKS:
Six Brides for Six Brothers

Dear Reader,

It's another white Christmas in Rust Creek Falls! Not a surprise to most of the town's residents, but a new experience for Wilder Crawford, who recently moved from Dallas with his father and five brothers.

The weather is only one of many things that are different this year. Another is the number of chairs at the table for the traditional holiday meal, as each of his siblings has got engaged or married since moving to Montana. Though Wilder is sincerely happy for each of them, the youngest Crawford brother has no intention of letting anyone lasso his heart.

Then the avowed bachelor gets an unexpected gift on Christmas Day: a four-month-old baby delivered to his door!

That baby is Beth Ames's nephew, and nothing matters more to Beth than family—especially little Cody. When she learns that the baby is in Rust Creek Falls, she immediately rushes to his side.

The cowboy and the schoolteacher have nothing in common, except their determination to do what is best for Cody. But the more time they spend together, the less their differences seem to matter. As they count down to December 31, an unexpected attraction starts to build, causing Wilder and Beth to wonder if the New Year could mean a new beginning for the three of them together—as a family.

I hope you enjoy Wilder and Beth's story.

Happy holidays!

Brenda Harlen

PS: Check out my website at brendaharlen.com or follow my Facebook page for up-to-date information about new and future releases.

Maverick Christmas Surprise

Brenda Harlen

Special thanks and acknowledgment are given to Brenda Harlen for her contribution to the Montana Mavericks: Six Brides for Six Brothers continuity.

ISBN-13: 978-1-335-57425-1

Maverick Christmas Surprise

This edition published by arrangement with Harlequin Books S.A.

For questions and comments about the quality of this book, please contact us at CustomerService@Harlequin.com.

Printed in U.S.A.

Brenda Harlen is a former attorney who once had the privilege of appearing before the Supreme Court of Canada. The practice of law taught her a lot about the world and reinforced her determination to become a writer—because in fiction, she could promise a happy ending! Now she is an award-winning, RITA® Award–nominated national bestselling author of more than thirty titles for Harlequin. You can keep up-to-date with Brenda on Facebook and Twitter or through her website, brendaharlen.com.

Books by Brenda Harlen

Harlequin Special Edition

Match Made in Haven

The Sheriff's Nine-Month Surprise
Her Seven-Day Fiancé
Six Weeks to Catch a Cowboy
Claiming the Cowboy's Heart
Double Duty for the Cowboy
One Night With the Cowboy

Montana Mavericks: The Lonelyhearts Ranch

Bring Me a Maverick for Christmas!

Montana Mavericks: The Great Family Roundup

The Maverick's Midnight Proposal

Visit the Author Profile page
at Harlequin.com for more titles.

To my MAC girls—Stacy, Freda, Elena & Jen—
with thanks for so many fabulous memories
(and in anticipation of many, many more!).

Prologue

Dallas, Texas
Christmas Eve

Beth Ames couldn't help but sing along with the holiday song on the radio. Christmas had always been her favorite time of the year, and she was even more excited this holiday season because it was her nephew's first. Four-month-old Cody was the love of her life, and she was grateful—if a little surprised—that her sister had invited her to celebrate the milestone occasion with them.

Over the years, the relationship between Beth and Leighton had been strained more often than not. While Beth might wish it wasn't so, she couldn't change the dynamic on her own, and her sister had always rebuffed her efforts to get closer. That had finally changed when Leighton confided to Beth that she was pregnant.

No doubt Leighton had been scared about the prospect of having and raising a child on her own, now that the baby's father was no longer a part of her life. Of course, Beth had questions about the man, but Leighton refused to answer them. And the more she pushed, the more her sister resisted.

"I appreciate your support, but I don't need your lectures," she'd said. "So if you want to be there with me when the baby is born, you'll stop asking about a guy who, I can assure you, has less than zero interest in being a dad."

Beth wondered how her sister could be so certain of his disinterest if she hadn't told him about her condition, but she bit her tongue. Because as much as she believed the father-to-be had a right to know, she didn't want to do anything to jeopardize their tentative truce.

Instead, Beth had focused on doing what she could to support Leighton throughout her pregnancy. She'd coached her during sixteen hours of labor, and she'd spent every free minute with the new mom and her baby during the first few weeks—until Leighton had recovered enough to demand some space.

Still, she understood that motherhood was a big adjustment for her usually vivacious and fun-loving sister, and she tried to help without stepping on the new mom's toes. But as the weeks turned into months, Leighton seemed increasingly worn out and unhappy.

Thankfully the onset of the Christmas season had revived her sister's good spirits. She'd been so genuinely filled with holiday spirit that she'd invited Beth to spend Christmas Eve at her apartment and even stay over to share in the morning celebration.

So now here she was, with her back seat full of festively wrapped presents and a box of groceries to prepare the holiday meal.

She didn't see her sister's car in its assigned parking spot, but it wouldn't be out of character for her to have forgotten something she needed to have before the stores closed. And since Leighton had given her a spare key, Beth didn't hesitate to let herself in so that she could put the perishables in the fridge.

After the groceries were away, she plugged in the Christmas tree lights and turned on the radio, tuning it to her favorite station that had been playing "all holiday music, all the time" since the first of December.

Feeling excited, and a little impatient, Beth decided to

call her sister to find out when she'd be home. She was surprised, when the phone started to ring, to hear an echo of the sound coming from the bedroom—where she discovered Leighton's cell plugged into the charger on the bedside table.

Shaking her head over her sister's forgetfulness, she started to turn away when she saw a note beside the charger with her name on it.

Beth,
Change of plans—sorry. I'll explain when I can.
Merry Christmas.
XO
L

Change of plans?

What the heck was *that* supposed to mean?

Where had her sister gone?

And, more important, *where was Cody*?

Chapter One

Rust Creek Falls, Montana
Christmas Day

And another one bites the dust, Wilder thought, listening to the excited chatter of conversation around the table as everyone congratulated Hunter and Merry on their engagement.

But he kept a smile on his face, because his brother was grinning, the bride-to-be was glowing and six-year-old Wren was ecstatic that her Christmas wish for a new mommy had come true. He was happy for Hunter and Merry and the new family they were making together, but he was also grateful that he wasn't shackled with the responsibilities of a wife or child.

Not that any of his siblings acted as if they were constrained by their relationships. In fact, his brothers Logan, Xander, Knox, Finn and now Hunter, too, seemed sincerely happy to have found a special someone to share their lives. But Wilder wasn't in any hurry to follow in their footsteps. He was perfectly happy with his life the way it was right now. As the old saying went, "if it ain't broke, don't fix it."

"I'm a lucky woman," Merry said, responding to a comment from one of her future brothers-in-law.

"And Hunter's a lucky man," Max said, about his newly engaged son.

Wilder couldn't help but notice that, in addition to the paternal pride on his father's face, there was a look of smug satisfaction. When the family had moved from Dallas to Rust Creek Falls six months earlier, Max had set out to find romantic matches for all of his sons—even going so far as to enlist the services of a local wedding planner to act as a matchmaker and offering her a million-dollar bonus if she succeeded. With the announcement of Hunter and Merry's engagement, he obviously felt as if he was well on his way to accomplishing his goal.

Five out of six was a pretty impressive success rate, Wilder acknowledged to himself. But his dad was doomed to disappointment if he expected to go six-for-six, because, at this point in his life, Wilder would rather be dead than wed.

"I'm lucky, too," Wren piped up, eager to be part of the conversation.

"You certainly are," Max agreed, and winked at his granddaughter before turning his attention back to the little girl's father and Hunter's fiancée. "And if there was any doubt about what was going on between you two, your daughter took care of that when she spilled the beans as soon as she ran into the house."

Wren's brow furrowed. "I didn't spill anything, Gramps," she said, obviously interpreting his remark literally. "I just said that Daddy's gonna marry Merry, and I get to be in the wedding and then she's gonna be my mom."

Yep, five out of six was impressive.

And now that five of his sons were happily settled, Max would no doubt focus all his attention on the sole remaining holdout.

Oh, hell.

Wilder didn't realize he'd spoken aloud until Hunter sternly admonished him with a single word: "Language."

"Sorry," he said, his apology automatic and sincere as he looked at each of the couples around the table.

"But I just realized that I'm the last Crawford bachelor standing."

His announcement of this uncomfortable truth was followed by several chuckles and teasing warnings from his siblings and their partners.

"I'm right there with you," Max pointed out to his youngest son.

"Says the man paying to get us all married off," Wilder noted dryly.

"Suck it up, kid," Finn said, with absolutely no sympathy in his tone. Because why should he feel sorry for his little brother? Finn was happily married to Avery and anticipating the birth of his first child with his bride of two months.

Then Finn shifted his attention to Hunter and Merry. "I guess this means that you two will be the next Crawford couple to take on the mysterious diary."

The book he was referring to had been discovered beneath a loose floorboard shortly after they'd moved into the two-story log home on the Ambling A Ranch. Apparently the "A" was for "Abernathy"—the name of the family who'd originally owned the property. A jewel-encrusted "A" was also on the front cover of the diary, suggesting the book had belonged to a member of the family.

Merry looked at her fiancé. "With everything going on, I almost forgot to tell you what I found out the night of Wren's play."

But whatever she'd learned would remain unknown to the rest of them a while longer, as an unexpected knock at the door interrupted her announcement.

Wilder's gaze moved around the table again, confirming that everyone who was supposed to be there for the family meal was present and accounted for.

So who the heck would be visiting on Christmas Day?

He pushed his chair away from the table to find out. Hunter stood at the same time, and the brothers made their way through the kitchen toward the source of the summons.

As Hunter opened the door, Wilder's attention was snagged by a blur of color on the driveway. By the time he registered that it was a red car, he was staring at taillights as the vehicle drove off. Fast. He squinted, trying to decipher the license plate, but the car was already too far away. The best he could do was to note that the plate was from Texas.

"I guess whoever knocked must have realized they were at the wrong place," he decided, despite a niggling feeling that he should have recognized the departing car.

"Or they did what they came here to do," his brother suggested.

Wilder glanced questioningly at Hunter, then followed the direction he was pointing and discovered an infant car seat on the porch—with a baby inside!

"What the—"

"There's a note." Hunter bent down to fish out a piece of paper pinned to the blue blanket wrapped around the sleeping baby.

He unfolded the page to reveal a handwritten message in a distinctly feminine scrawl and began to read aloud:

"'Wilder—'" he glanced up from the page to give his brother a quizzical look before continuing "'—this is your baby. I've done the best I could for four months and I can't do it anymore. A boy needs a dad and you're Cody's, so it's your turn now. Please take good care of him.' It's signed 'L.'"

He looked at Wilder again. "Well, little brother, looks like you got a baby for Christmas."

Wilder snatched the paper out of Hunter's hand to read it for himself.

His brother said something else, but Wilder didn't hear him.

He stared at the writing on the page, as if he could will the words to change—or at least make sense of them. But none of this made any sense to him. It simply wasn't possible that he was the father of this kid.

Was it?

"What's going on out here?" Max wanted to know, pushing his way between his sons. "Good Lord…it's a baby."

"Wilder's baby," Hunter said and, miming the act of washing his hands, retreated into the house where the rest of the family was gathered.

His father pinned Wilder with his gaze. "You want to explain this?"

"I wish I could," he said. "But I've never seen the kid before. I'm as shocked by this as you are."

"But it's yours," his father remarked.

It wasn't a question.

"That's what the note says," Wilder acknowledged.

"You don't believe it?" Max asked him.

"I don't know what to believe. What to think." He scrubbed a hand over his face, sincerely baffled by this turn of events. He wanted to believe it was a joke, though he wasn't the least bit amused. "Who would abandon their kid on somebody's doorstep in the middle of winter?"

"Not just *somebody's* doorstep," his father argued. "The baby's father's doorstep."

He shook his head. "It's not possible."

"You've never been intimate with a woman?" Max challenged.

It was, of course, a rhetorical question. Though Wilder didn't share details of his romantic encounters, he'd been caught—more than once—sneaking into the house the morning after he'd spent the night in a woman's bed.

"I'm careful," he assured his father. *"Always."*

"Accidents happen," Max said matter-of-factly.

It was a terrifying thought.

"The note says he's four months old," his father continued. "Adding nine months to that is thirteen, which means the baby would have been conceived sometime around November last year."

"Okay," Wilder said hesitantly.

"So who were you with last November?" Max pressed.

Last November? *Seriously?*

He shrugged. "How am I supposed to remember something that happened that far back?"

Which he immediately realized was *not* the right thing to say to his father under the circumstances.

"You should darn well remember a woman who shared your bed," Max said, the low tone of his voice doing nothing to disguise the underlying anger and disappointment. "I don't expect you to be in love with every woman you sleep with, but you should know and respect her enough to remember her name."

"Give me a break," Wilder pleaded. "My head's spinning so fast, it's a wonder I know my own name right now."

"Well, there's no doubt the baby looks like a Crawford."

"The baby looks like a baby," Wilder said. Because in his admittedly limited experience with infants, they all looked like bald, chubby-cheeked, squalling little monsters.

As if on cue, the one buckled into the car seat started to squirm and squall.

Wilder stepped back, an instinctive retreat.

"Pick him up and bring him inside," Max said.

"Me?" Wilder was horrified by the very thought.

With a sigh, his father reached down and grabbed the

car seat with one hand and the enormous diaper bag with the other.

"Hunter said there was a baby on the doorstep," Avery said, entering the kitchen from the dining room at the same time that Wilder and Max came in from the porch.

Then she spotted the carrier in Max's hand and her expression softened. "Ohmygod—it *is* a baby." Her gaze shifted to Wilder. "Why didn't you tell anyone you're a daddy?"

"Because I'm *not*," Wilder insisted. "There's no way that kid's mine."

"He's in denial," Genevieve, his brother Knox's wife, said. Because apparently Hunter's announcement had drawn everyone away from the table.

"I think the baby's hungry," Lily said worriedly.

"You just want to feed everyone," her husband Xander teased.

"He is gnawing on his fist," Hunter noted. "And that's a telltale sign of hunger."

As Hunter was the only one of his brothers with significant daddy experience, Wilder was willing to defer to his expertise. But having the problem identified didn't give him the first clue about how to solve it.

So when his brothers and their partners—and Wren—huddled around the baby, pushing Wilder and Max out of the way, Wilder didn't object.

"He's definitely hungry," Sarah said, as the baby's unhappy cries turned to sobs.

"Let's see if there's a bottle in the bag," Merry suggested.

There were, in fact, two bottles—one premixed and one empty, plus a can of powdered formula.

Avery unbuckled the harness and lifted the infant out of his seat. His plaintive cries immediately ceased.

Everyone seemed to be talking at once, speculating

about the note as they fussed over the little guy. Wilder took advantage of their preoccupation to study the baby—who didn't seem quite so intimidating now that he was quiet—and realized, a little uneasily, that the baby was staring back at him.

Is it possible? he wondered. *Can he be mine?*

"Where'd the baby come from?" Wren wanted to know.

"Someone left him on the doorstep," her dad explained.

"Maybe he's a gift from Santa," she suggested.

Hunter chuckled. "Unfortunately for Uncle Wilder, I don't think the baby came with a gift receipt."

"He does look a lot like Wilder's old baby photos," Logan, the eldest Crawford brother, noted.

"He does not," Wilder denied, though without much conviction.

But no one was paying any attention to him, anyway.

Except his father, who sidled closer. "The note was signed with the letter 'L,'" Max noted. "Does that jog your memory at all?"

He automatically started to shake his head, because he didn't want his memory jogged. And if he was in denial—well, he was quite happy to stay there. Because in denial, his life was easy and carefree and he didn't have the responsibility of an infant who'd been dumped into his lap—or, to be more precise, on his doorstep.

But somehow, in the midst of all the chaos going on around him, hazy memories slowly came into focus in Wilder's mind. Memories of an early holiday party at Reunion Tower in Dallas, a few too many cocktails and a pretty—and very adventurous—blonde named Leighton Ames. And no, he wasn't oblivious to the fact that her name started with the same letter that had been scrawled on the bottom of the note.

They'd had a good time together, not just that night, but

for several weeks afterward. And then, just as suddenly as their relationship had started, it ended.

Her decision, Wilder remembered now.

Just after the New Year, she'd abruptly called things off. He'd been a little disappointed at first, but there were plenty of other women in the world. And truthfully, he hadn't thought of her again—until now.

Was Leighton the baby's mother?

Was it possible that he *was* the father of this baby who'd been abandoned on the doorstep?

But if she believed that to be true, why hadn't she ever told him that she was pregnant?

Well, he could probably guess the answer to that one. Either Leighton wasn't sure about the baby's paternity, or she didn't trust him to step up.

He would have, of course. He would have undoubtedly felt panicked and trapped, but he would have done the right thing. Not that she could have known that, because they hadn't had the type of relationship where they talked about their future hopes and dreams. Their conversations had been more along the lines of "your place or mine?" And after that question had been answered, there had been even less talking.

But if she hadn't trusted him to step up, why would she dump the baby on him now?

And how did she even know where to find him?

He'd had no communication with her in almost a year. And the last time they were together, he didn't know that he'd be moving to Rust Creek Falls, so it was unlikely she could have tracked him down here.

Reassured by his own reasoning that it couldn't have been Leighton who dropped the baby off—and conveniently ignoring the fact that his name was on the note—Wilder breathed a sigh of relief, confident that he was off the hook. But his father would require additional proof, so as the rest of the family went back into the dining room, he scrolled through the contacts in his phone to see if he still had her number.

Amazingly, he did, and tapped it to initiate the call.

"Hello?"

The female voice that immediately answered sounded frantic.

"Um...hi," he said. "I'm trying to reach Leighton Ames."

"You and me both," she replied, sounding as if she was fighting tears.

He frowned at that. "Is this still her number?"

"Yes, but she forgot her phone when she left." The woman on the other end of the line sighed. "Or maybe she didn't forget it."

Which didn't make any sense to him, but all he said was: "Well, if you hear from her, can you ask her to call Wilder Crawford?"

"Why?" She sounded both curious and wary. "What business do you have with my sister?"

Sister?

He couldn't recall Leighton mentioning a sister, but surely a sister would know if Leighton had had a baby. And if this was Leighton's baby, that meant the woman on the phone was the baby's aunt.

Before he could ask, she spoke again. "Wait a minute—did you say Wilder Crawford?"

"I did," he confirmed.

"I found your name and a Montana address scrawled on a Post-it note in Leighton's apartment," she said. "I think she might be on her way to see you."

The knots in his stomach tightened. "She might have been here already...and left something."

He heard a sharp intake of breath. "What kind of something?"

"A baby," he admitted. "Did she—"

"Cody!" she immediately interjected, not giving him a chance to finish. "You have Cody?"

"That's the name in the note," he confirmed.

"Note?" she echoed.

"The baby was left on my doorstep with a note."

"I don't understand. Why would she leave her baby?"

"I wish I knew," he told her.

"Are you Cody's father?" she guessed.

"Obviously your sister thinks so."

"You haven't seen her or talked to her?"

"Not in the past year."

"But Cody's with you? At the Ambling A Ranch in Montana?"

"That's right," he confirmed.

"Okay. I'll be there as soon as I can," she promised.

"Wait—"

But she'd already disconnected the call.

"What did you find out?" Max asked, when Wilder returned to the table where Lily had resumed serving dessert and Avery rocked the now quiet baby.

"The kid's mom is Leighton Ames," he said. "I spoke to her sister, but she doesn't know where she is or why she left the baby here."

"Because she wanted him to be with his dad," Max suggested as an answer to the latter question.

Wilder hoped like hell his father was wrong.

"Do you want ice cream with your pie?" Merry asked him.

Because for the rest of the family gathered together, today was still a celebration—and it was time for dessert.

"Sure," he said.

Though he wasn't even sure he wanted the pie now, he didn't want his family to know how freaked out he was about the arrival of the baby they were all happy enough to assume was his and turning down dessert would be a definite red flag.

"I want ice cream," Wren piped up, pushing her bowl toward her soon-to-be-stepmother who was scooping it.

"You already had ice cream," her dad reminded her, pulling the bowl back again before Merry could indulge the little girl's request.

Wren pouted and dragged her spoon around the inside of the empty vessel.

Wilder took the plate Merry passed to him and murmured his thanks. Then he halved the scoop of ice cream with the side of his fork and slid half into his niece's bowl.

Wren beamed at him; Hunter scowled.

"There's a reason I'm the favorite uncle," he said, and winked at the little girl.

"I'm finished with my dessert," Finn said to his wife then, "if you want me to take the baby."

"I can manage the baby," Avery assured him. "If you want to be helpful, you can start clearing the table."

As Finn began gathering empty plates and glasses, Wilder dug his fork into his pie, giving up the pretense of an appetite.

"Did you ask for a baby for Christmas, Uncle Wilder?" his niece asked, around a mouthful of ice cream.

"No." His response was immediate and definitive.

"I guess you're just lucky then," Wren decided.

Lucky?

Oh yeah, he had a horseshoe so far up his butt he couldn't swallow the pie that was stuck in his throat.

The house emptied quickly after dessert was finished and the cleanup complete, leaving Wilder and his father alone with the baby. Then Max took off, too, to pick up a crib he'd arranged to borrow from one of their many Crawford relatives in town.

Wilder had offered to make the trip, but his dad had insisted that he stay at the Ambling A to watch the baby. For the first half hour, there weren't any major snags—because the kid slept. But when he woke up, he was not in a very good mood.

The baby didn't cry. Not really. But his face was all scrunched up and he was squirming in his seat, and Wilder braced himself for the crying to start.

"Avery promised that you would sleep for a few hours," Wilder said, trying to reason with the infant. "That was barely more than an hour ago."

His words got the kid's attention, though, and he fixed his big, blue eyes on Wilder.

"You can't be hungry already," he continued, in the same logical tone. "You sucked back a whole bottle before she left."

The baby continued to fuss, clearly unconvinced and unhappy.

And his lower lip was starting to do that quivering thing that warned Wilder real tears and sobs likely weren't too far behind.

"I'm sorry," he said. "But I don't know what to do."

"You could try picking him up."

Wilder turned to see Hunter standing in the doorway. "I thought you'd gone home."

"I did," his brother confirmed. "And then I came back."

"Why?"

"Because I thought you might want to talk to someone who's been where you are."

On another day, Wilder might have made a snarky comment about not remembering when a baby had been left on Hunter's doorstep, but right now, he was too grateful for his presence to risk saying anything that might prompt him to leave again.

"I think I need a manual more than a sounding board," he confided.

"A manual would be useless," Hunter said. "Because every baby is different."

"So how am I supposed to know what's wrong with this one?"

"He's probably out of sorts because he doesn't know where his mama is."

"That makes two of us," Wilder said.

"And when babies are out of sorts, they need to be comforted."

He gestured to the infant in his carrier. "Feel free."

But his brother shook his head. "You need to step up."

"I would have stepped up months ago if Leighton had told me she was pregnant," he said in his defense.

"So why are you hesitating now?" his brother challenged.

"Because I don't have the first clue what to do with a baby."

"No first-time parent has a clue in the beginning."

His brother's matter-of-fact statement was hardly reassuring.

And while they were talking, the baby was growing more distressed.

With a sigh of resignation, Wilder unhooked the strap and lifted him out of the seat.

The baby stopped fussing for a moment to stare at him, as if waiting for something else.

Something more.

Wilder looked at his brother. "I'm doing this wrong, aren't I?"

"Babies generally like to be held closer than arm's length," Hunter told him.

Wilder pulled his arms toward his chest, so that he was almost nose-to-nose with the kid.

Hunter started to chuckle, but quickly covered it with a cough when Wilder glared at him.

"Closer," he urged. "But to the side, with his head about level with your shoulder so he can see behind you. With newborns, you need to keep one hand on the bottom and the other on the head and neck, for support, but he's obviously strong enough to hold his head up just fine."

Wilder did his best to follow his brother's instructions.

"That's it," Hunter assured him.

"He feels so tiny." His whispered remark was filled with awe and wonder—and just a hint of the nerves that were tangled up inside him. "So fragile."

"It's normal to be scared. I was terrified the first time I held Wren in my arms," his brother confided. "And she was a lot smaller than Cody is."

"But you had nine months to prepare yourself for her arrival," Wilder pointed out, though he wasn't sure anything could have prepared him for this moment.

Hunter nodded. "True."

Wilder patted the baby's back gently, as he'd watched Sarah do, and was rewarded with a shockingly loud belch.

"Gas might have been another cause of his distress," Hunter noted then.

"You think?" Wilder asked dryly.

"And now that it's out of his system, you can try the cradle hold," he said, and talked him through shifting the baby's position so that he was tucked in the crook of Wilder's arm. "Now sit down and relax."

Relax? He wasn't sure he'd be able to relax so long as there was a baby under his roof.

And though Leighton's note had given no indication that she was planning to come back for the little guy, he had to believe that she would. After all, what kind of mom just left her kid?

Mine, he thought, then shoved the unpleasant twinge from his mind.

Hunter took another seat at the table, leaning back in the chair and stretching his legs out in front.

Obviously relaxing wasn't a problem for him.

"Where'd Dad go?" he asked.

"To pick up a crib," Wilder told him.

"Ah, right. He said he was going to try to rustle up some of the stuff you'd need from local relatives," his brother recalled.

"Unfortunately, I don't think one of those things is a nanny."

Hunter chuckled. "No, he's been pretty clear that your baby is your responsibility."

"But we don't even know for sure that he is my baby," Wilder felt compelled to point out again.

"Obviously his mom is sure. Though I have to wonder, if you haven't kept in touch with her, how did she know where to find you?"

"I've been wondering the same thing. My best guess is Malcolm," Wilder said, naming a close buddy from Dallas. "When I talked to him a few weeks back, he'd mentioned that one of the girls we'd met at the holiday party before Christmas last year had shown up at his office to ask about me. But he told me that before Thanksgiving, and since nothing came of it..."

"Until now," Hunter remarked.

"Until now," he agreed.

"So the who and the how have been answered," his brother noted. "But we still don't know the why—beyond the obvious, of course."

"What's the obvious?" Wilder wondered.

"What 'L' wrote in her note—a boy needs a dad."

"Which proves she doesn't know me at all, or she'd know I'm not dad material."

"Or maybe she knows you better than you know yourself," Hunter suggested. "But since I'm not completely without sympathy, I'll give you a crash course in diapering and feeding."

"I can hardly wait," he said dryly.

"Or I can let you figure it out on your own," his brother suggested as an alternative.

"Please don't," he said, immediately remorseful. "I need all the help I can get."

"You're doing okay so far," Hunter assured him.

"Because I'm not doing anything."

"You've managed to relax," his brother pointed out. "And that's allowed Cody to relax, too."

Wilder looked down at the little guy tucked in the crook of his arm, close to his body.

He did look relaxed. Content even, his eyelids heavy, as if he might—fingers crossed—drift off to sleep again. And Wilder felt a small measure of satisfaction that he'd been the one to put that look on his face, though the satisfaction wasn't nearly strong enough to quell the rising tide of panic within him.

"I'm not ready for this," he confided. "I figured I had another ten years of footloose and fancy-free living before I even thought about getting serious with a woman—and then a few more after that before I had to worry about becoming a dad."

"There's nothing more serious than parenthood, or more amazing and awe-inspiring," Hunter told him.

The baby turned his head then, rubbing his cheek against the soft plaid of Wilder's shirt, just about where he felt his heart swell inside his chest.

And Wilder knew that whatever happened next, he and the kid were in this together.

Chapter Two

Beth turned up the radio and lowered the window a couple of inches, just far enough to allow the icy December air to sweep through the interior of her car and jolt her weary brain and sleepy body awake. Eager to get to Rust Creek Falls, she'd left Dallas almost immediately after ending her telephone conversation with Wilder Crawford, making only brief stops to fill her gas tank and use the bathroom. Now, after almost twenty-eight hours on the road, she was tired and hungry but refused to give in to either before she reached her final destination—and Cody.

She'd looked into flights to Montana, but the last-minute airfares and required connections made it more logical to drive. And now her journey was finally nearing its end.

She couldn't wait to see Cody again, to hold his chubby little body in her arms and breathe in his sweet baby powder scent. She'd been so worried when she found Leighton's note, but after talking to Wilder Crawford, she had reason to believe the baby was okay. She had no clue about her sister. Though Leighton had always been adept at taking care of herself, she hadn't quite been herself since the baby was born. Maybe it wasn't Beth's place to worry about her sister, but of course she *was* worried. And she was concerned that her sweet and innocent nephew was being used as a pawn in whatever game his mother was playing.

When Beth realized her sister was gone—likely headed

to Montana, where one of the previously unidentified potential fathers of her baby apparently now resided—she'd considered that Leighton might want to reconcile with her ex. And she'd hoped, for Cody's sake, that was her sister's plan.

But if what Wilder Crawford had told her was true, Leighton hadn't even spoken to the man in almost a year. So why would her sister travel all this way and then not see him? And why would she abandon her baby on his doorstep without any warning?

Maybe Leighton had decided that she needed a break from the day-to-day responsibilities of caring for Cody. But why not leave him in Dallas with his aunt? Why drive all the way to Middle-of-Nowhere, Montana—in the middle of winter, no less—and leave him with a stranger?

Even more than those questions baffled Beth's brain, the insult wounded her heart. She'd made every effort to be there for Leighton since she'd learned of her sister's pregnancy. She'd tried to offer support without judgment, help without expectation. And she'd cried tears of joy along with her sister when Cody drew his first breath—and let it out again as an indignant wail.

Beth would do anything for her nephew—including driving through the night and all the next day to get to him. Unfortunately she hadn't considered the changes in weather that she would encounter en route, and the tires on her fuel-efficient hatchback had been slipping and sliding in protest against the snow and ice that had been her near constant companion since Colorado Springs.

But according to the faded "Welcome to Rust Creek Falls" sign posted at the side the highway, she had finally arrived. She checked her speed as she drove down Cedar Street, noting that the storefronts were all decked out for the holidays with boughs of evergreen and big red bows and twinkling lights. Of course, it was late on the day after

Christmas, so the stores were closed, the roads mostly empty. No doubt all the town's residents were huddled comfortably in their homes, basking in the holiday afterglow and enjoying time with family and friends.

Certainly that was how she'd anticipated spending her holiday—not driving 1700 miles on her own, worry growing with each tick of the odometer. But missing out on the holiday didn't matter right now. All that mattered was Cody.

Once she was reunited with her nephew, she would think about how to track down her sister. Or maybe—fingers crossed—Leighton had already decided to return to Rust Creek Falls to pick up her baby and Beth would find her sister at the Ambling A when she arrived.

Continuing to follow the directions on her phone, she finally pulled into a long, winding drive that would supposedly lead her to the Ambling A. Assuming, of course, that her GPS wasn't sending her into the middle of a field where she'd get stuck in the snow and find herself surrounded by angry cows.

The drive had been plowed, but it was still snow-covered, making everything appear blindingly white when her headlights cut through the blackness of the night. She drove slowly, carefully, following the tire tracks to ensure she didn't veer off the road and end up in a ditch.

The dash clock read 10:14 when she finally saw the two-story log home. Parking behind a dark pickup, she felt a slight twinge of disappointment that she didn't see Leighton's car, but right now her main focus was Cody.

Still, she gave herself a moment to close her eyes that were burning with strain and fatigue. But only a moment, because any longer than that and she wasn't sure she'd manage to open them again. And anyway, as exhausted as she was, her nephew was inside that house, and she couldn't wait a minute longer to see him.

Grabbing her purse, she pushed open the door. The blast of frigid air was a stark reminder that she wasn't in Dallas anymore. Stepping out of the car, she nearly lost her footing on the snow-covered ground as the short-heeled boots that were perfectly suitable for winter in Texas proved to be no match for the ice and snow of Montana.

She blinked in the sudden brightness as a floodlight activated. A motion sensor, she guessed, grateful for the illumination as she moved carefully over the frozen ground.

There were no lights on inside the house, but she wasn't going to let that stop her now.

She noted the pine boughs draped over the railing of the porch and an enormous evergreen wreath decorated with a fancy velvet bow on the door—more reminders of the holiday she'd missed celebrating. She climbed the porch steps and, after a moment's hesitation, bypassed the bell to knock on the door instead.

When there was no response, she knocked a little harder.

Then harder again.

Finally, a light came on overhead, the door was wrenched open from the other side, and Beth found herself face-to-face with an obviously irritated man.

Actually, she was face-to-chest with his gray T-shirt, so she didn't see the scowl that furrowed his brow until she took an instinctive step back and lifted her gaze to his face.

In addition to the scowl, he was wearing a pair of flannel pajama bottoms low on his hips and the previously noted T-shirt that stretched across his muscular torso. He folded strong arms over his broad chest now and pinned her with a dark, piercing gaze, causing her to belatedly question the wisdom of showing up at a stranger's door on an isolated ranch in the middle of the night.

Because she was certain that the sudden dryness of her throat and pounding of her heart were signs of fear and not an immediate and instinctive attraction to the prime male specimen in front of her.

"I don't know where you're from, honey, but 'round here, people don't come visiting in the middle of the night," he said.

The growly timbre of his voice made her shiver.

Or maybe it was just the frigid air temperature.

"Dallas," Beth heard herself respond to what was obviously a rhetorical question. "And I'm not visiting—I'm here for my nephew."

"You're the woman who answered Leighton's phone," he concluded.

"Lisbeth," she said. "But most people call me Beth. And you must be Wilder."

He nodded and, after only a moment's hesitation, stepped away from the door to allow her to enter.

She had a vague impression of a kitchen beyond the entranceway, though the interior was only dimly illuminated by the light that filtered through the window from the porch. She kicked off her boots and left them on the mat by the door and unbuttoned her thin coat as she followed Wilder further into a house that was toasty warm in contrast to the frigid air outside. "Where's Cody?"

She sensed more than saw his frown this time. "Did your sister send you to get him?"

In retrospect, Beth would acknowledge that she should have answered his question with a firm and decisive *yes*. But in her agitated and sleep-deprived state, she wasn't thinking clearly enough to see the obvious solution to her dilemma.

"No, I still haven't heard from Leighton," she admitted instead. "And I'm starting to worry that something might have happened to her."

"I think what happened is that she got tired of being

tied down by a baby," he said, and handed her a piece of paper that he'd retrieved from the table.

As she unfolded the page, he turned on the light over the stove so that she'd be able to read it. Beth immediately recognized her sister's handwriting, and her heart sank as she skimmed the brief words. Then she read them more carefully.

"I don't understand," she said, after she'd scanned the note a third time.

"That makes two of us."

She looked at him again, noting the stubble that darkened his jaw and the overlong and tousled hair that suggested he'd just crawled out of bed. He was undeniably sexy with a slightly dangerous edge—exactly her sister's type.

None of which explained why she felt a quiver low in her belly when she found him looking back at her. Of course, it was probably just that she was overtired and overwhelmed and worried about her nephew. It certainly wasn't a visceral response to his nearness. It couldn't be.

She cleared her throat as she refolded the note and handed it back to Wilder. "I want to see Cody now. Please."

He hesitated, and for a moment, she thought he might refuse. But maybe he sensed that she wouldn't be put off—and that, if he even tried, she'd raise enough ruckus to wake the whole house—because he finally nodded.

She followed him through the darkness, up a set of stairs, then down a hall until he finally paused in an open doorway. She glanced past him, into a room dimly illuminated by a nightlight plugged in beside a crib.

"It looks like maybe you were expecting him," she noted.

He shook his head. "Maggie and Jesse—distant but local relatives—loaned us the crib. And the rocking chair."

Beth tiptoed to the crib, exhaling a long, quiet sigh of relief when she gazed down at the sleeping baby.

"It's okay, Cody. I'm here to take you home now." She murmured the words softly as she reached down to lift him into her arms and cuddle him against her chest. He squirmed a little at first, but settled quickly again without making a sound of protest.

Wilder stepped in front of the door, as if to block her path, and crossed those strong arms over his impressive chest again. "What are you talking about?" Though he kept his volume low so as not to disturb the sleeping infant, there was no mistaking the steel in his words. "You're not going anywhere with that baby."

"Of course, I am," she said. "I'm his aunt. He belongs with me."

"If his mother believed that, why'd she drive halfway across the country to bring him to me?" he challenged.

Beth faltered. "I don't know. But my sister's done a lot of things in her life that I can't begin to fathom."

"Well, it seems obvious to me that there must be a reason Leighton didn't want you caring for her baby."

"*Her* baby?" she echoed. "You don't think he's your baby, too?"

"I don't know what to think," he admitted. "But I know that it's late and this conversation should be tabled until the morning."

"Morning?" she echoed. "I expected to be halfway back to Dallas by morning."

"When was the last time you slept, Lisbeth?"

"It's Beth," she corrected automatically. "And…I'm not sure."

He nodded. "That's what I figured." He pointed to the rocking chair beside the crib. "Sit there with the baby for a few minutes while I make up the bed in the spare room across the hall."

"Oh. Um…thank you."

She hadn't expected an invitation to stay. Of course,

his words had been more in the nature of a command than an offer, but still, she was grateful. So she lowered herself into the rocking chair and snuggled with her nephew.

There were no words to express how happy she was to have Cody in her arms again, how grateful she was to know that he was safe. Worry and desperation had fueled her throughout the trip from Dallas—along with regular infusions of caffeine. But now that she was here, she felt completely drained—physically and emotionally.

She was also relieved that she didn't have to drive any further tonight, even if it was just back into town to rent a room at a local motel. Assuming there was a motel in this town.

In any event, it probably wasn't a bad idea for her to catch some shut-eye before embarking on the return journey.

It didn't take Wilder long to put sheets on the bed in the guest room. And yet, he wasn't surprised to return to the spare room that had been turned into a temporary nursery to find Beth fast asleep in the rocking chair, her nephew still in her arms.

Though he had no reason to doubt her claim that she was Leighton's sister, he couldn't see any obvious family resemblance. Leighton was a spirited blonde, and his first impression of Lisbeth was of a solemn brunette. With her messy ponytail and shapeless coat, Beth bore no physical resemblance to her curvy sister with the infectious laugh and lust for life.

And yet, there was something about Beth that sparked an unexpected—and unwanted—awareness inside him. Or maybe it was her obvious connection to her nephew that tugged at him. She'd wasted no time in making the trip from Dallas to Rust Creek Falls when she learned that he was there, which made him wonder again why Leighton had made the same trip to leave her baby with him when she had a sister who obviously would have been happy to care for the kid.

Unfortunately, he wasn't going to get an answer to that question—or any other questions—tonight. So he reached for the baby, intending to return him to the crib. Beth's arms instinctively tightened around the baby and her eyes flew open—a warrior ready to battle.

"I'm just putting him back in his bed so that you can go to yours," he told her.

She blinked, and he noticed then that she had really pretty eyes—the color of dark chocolate and fringed by a sweep of long, dark lashes.

Those lashes fluttered again as the confusion slowly cleared from her gaze. "Oh. Okay." She whispered her response as she finally relinquished her hold. "I guess I'm more tired than I realized."

"You can sleep now," he said, as she rose from the chair.

She nodded. "Thank you. For letting me stay here tonight."

He didn't point out that the offer had been born of necessity rather than kindness, because he couldn't have her knocking on the door of Strickland's Boarding House at this late hour. And the only other option nearby was Maverick Manor, but he'd heard the owner proudly remark that the hotel was fully booked through the holidays.

"Go." He steered her toward the open doorway across the hall. "There's an unopened toothbrush and toothpaste in the adjoining bathroom, if you need them."

"Thank you," she said again.

He turned back to peek at the baby again, exhaling a weary sigh of relief that the little guy was still sleeping soundly—at least for the moment—before starting toward his own room.

Thanks to the attention and efforts of his family, the baby had been well cared for the previous day. But eventually they'd all headed back to their own homes, leaving Wilder and his dad alone with the infant.

As a father of six boys, Max had had more than his fair share of experience with diapers and bottles, but he'd insisted that this baby was his youngest son's responsibility. Wilder didn't think it was fair that his father was willing to assume that he was the kid's dad just because some woman had scrawled his name at the top of the note.

"And because you admitted that you had a relationship with the mother," Max had explained, when Wilder challenged the assumption of paternity.

He couldn't deny that argument had some merit. That it wasn't entirely outside the realm of possibility that he could be the father.

And that possibility scared the bejeezus out of him.

And if Leighton had paused long enough to consider the implications of that possibility before depositing her child at his door, it would have scared the bejeezus out of her, too.

What had she been thinking?

Unfortunately, the answer to that question was probably that she *hadn't* been thinking.

By her own admission, she wasn't much of a planner. It was more fun, she'd once told him, to live in the moment and embrace whatever surprises life had in store for her.

When Wilder had confided that he wasn't a big fan of surprises, she'd surprised the heck out of him by inviting him back to her place.

And yeah, he'd liked *that* surprise.

This "surprise, you're a daddy" thing—not so much.

And if he really was the kid's dad…well, he couldn't help but feel sorry for the little guy, because there was no chance Wilder was ever going to win a "Father of the Year" award.

Chapter Three

Beth didn't remember her head hitting the pillow.

She fell asleep quickly and slept deeply, and when she opened her eyes again, the clock on the bedside table read 12:48 p.m.

Certain that number couldn't be accurate, she pressed the button on the side of her watch to illuminate its face.

12:48.

She jolted upright, shocked to realize that she'd slept for almost fourteen hours!

Her first thought after that: *Cody.*

She immediately pushed back the covers and hurried across the hall. Her heart, which had been pounding furiously against her ribs, settled into a more normal rhythm when she found her nephew in the crib, sleeping soundly.

She didn't believe for a minute that he was *still* sleeping. More likely, Cody had been up at 6 a.m.—as was his habit—and was now down for his second nap of the day. And because he was napping, she decided to steal a few more minutes for herself and indulge in a hot shower.

And it was an indulgence. She had no idea how old or new the house was, but it was apparent that the bathroom had been recently renovated with a mosaic tile floor and glass-walled shower. She stood for a long time beneath the rainfall shower head, letting the warm water wash over her body, easing the tension and aches in her muscles.

She used the shampoo and bodywash in the enclosure, as her own toiletries were in the duffel bag that she'd left in her car. Which meant that the change of clothes she'd packed for her overnight stay at her sister's apartment was still in the car, too.

As she wrapped herself in a thick, fluffy towel from the heated rack, she considered that ranching was obviously a much more lucrative profession than teaching. Not that she'd ever trade her class of kindergarteners for a field of cows, but she suspected that her sister might not have been so quick to discount the idea of spending her life with a cowboy if she'd known Wilder was a wealthy cowboy.

Of course, thinking about Leighton led to worrying about Leighton, even though Beth knew it was an exercise in futility. She had no way of getting in touch with her sister, so all she could do was monitor her social media accounts, check in with her friends and wait for Leighton to contact her—and ensure that Cody was taken care of while he waited for his mom to come back.

Because Leighton *would* come back. Notwithstanding what she'd written in the note she'd left with Cody, Beth knew that her sister wouldn't abandon her baby. She loved him too much.

Reassured by this internal pep talk, Beth toweled off and got dressed in her old clothes. As she finished towel-drying her hair, she heard voices across the hall in her nephew's temporary bedroom.

No, only one voice, she realized.

Deep and masculine, murmuring in a quiet tone.

Wilder's voice.

Her heart skipped a beat then, as it had the night before when he'd appeared in the door: six-feet-plus of rugged masculinity that, even in her worried and sleep-deprived state, she couldn't help but respond to.

She'd had two brief conversations with him: the first on the telephone, when he'd called looking for Leighton, and the second last night, when she'd arrived at the ranch, unannounced and uninvited. Although she should have been expected, as she'd told him she'd be on her way to Rust Creek Falls to get her nephew as soon as possible. Regardless, Wilder had been more hospitable than she'd had any right to expect.

Or maybe he'd been relieved to see her. Because standing in the doorway of the room across the hall, it was obvious to Beth that this cowboy had absolutely no clue how to take care of a baby.

"I know you can't do this on your own," Wilder said to the baby. "But is it too much to ask for just a little bit of cooperation?"

Of course Cody didn't respond, and Beth stayed quiet, too, watching as Wilder struggled to get the baby's legs out of his sleeper, opting to stretch the fabric rather than attempt to bend his limbs.

When that was finally done, he unsnapped the fasteners of the onesie and peeled it back to reveal the diaper.

"Or maybe this is some kind of test that only someone worthy of being called Mommy or Daddy can figure out," Wilder considered, as he opened the Velcro tabs. "And I think it's pretty obvious to both of us by now that I'm not worthy."

Beth wanted to say something then, to reassure the handsome cowboy that everyone struggled with parenting tasks in the beginning. But before she could find the right words, he pulled the diaper away and reached down to retrieve a clean one from the bag on the floor.

Cody responded as most baby boys would when his private parts were exposed to the fresh air, and Wilder yelped in surprise at the stream that fountained into the air.

Beth couldn't help it—she laughed.

The sound caught the attention of Cody and Wilder, and they both turned to the doorway. But while the baby smiled in recognition, the man looked so miserably unhappy she couldn't help but feel sorry for him, at least a little.

She swallowed another chuckle as she stepped into the room. "Is this your first time changing a diaper?"

"No," he denied, and blew out a breath. "I just don't expect him to do that every single time."

"You need to keep baby boys covered," she told him.

"How am I supposed to keep him covered *and* change his diaper?" Wilder grumbled, rummaging through the bag again.

"It isn't that difficult," she said. "You just don't remove the wet diaper until you have a dry one ready."

He sighed wearily and shoved the diaper bag aside. "And apparently that was the last clean undershirt thing."

"I packed some things for Cody before I left Leighton's apartment," Beth said. "But the bag's still on the passenger seat in my car."

"If you don't mind keeping an eye on him for a few minutes, I'll go get it for you," Wilder said.

"The keys are in my coat pocket," she told him.

He nodded. "I'll be right back."

While he was gone, she stripped Cody out of his damp clothes and put a clean diaper on him, chatting with him the whole while. Or chatting *to* him, as her nephew didn't respond except with happy gurgles and excited kicks. But those were enough for Beth to know that he was glad to see her.

After wrapping Cody in a blanket to keep him warm until Wilder returned, she sat with him in the rocking chair and rummaged through the diaper bag.

"It doesn't look like your mama thought to pack you any toys or books," she remarked. "Hopefully that's because she doesn't plan on being gone for too long."

Although the note Leighton had written suggested otherwise, Beth refused to believe that her sister would leave

Cody for more than a few days. It was more likely, she reasoned, that her sister had made the trip to Montana so that Cody could meet his dad, and the long journey with the baby had pushed her beyond the limits of her patience.

But Beth still didn't understand what had compelled her sister to contact the man now. Or why she hadn't mentioned her plans to Beth. Especially when they'd made arrangements to celebrate Cody's first Christmas together.

"I couldn't imagine any reason she would want to bring you to Montana," Beth admitted. "But now that I've met the very handsome cowboy who might be your daddy, I think I'm beginning to understand."

"So you *do* think I'm handsome."

Beth glanced up then to see Wilder in the doorway, a cocky grin on his face, and felt her cheeks burn.

"It's not my opinion so much as a simple fact," she said, furiously attempting to backpedal from her own admission.

"But attraction is very much subjective," he pointed out.

"I didn't say I was attracted to you," she denied hotly. "I was merely commenting that I could understand why *my sister* was attracted to you."

"Sure. We'll go with that," he said, as he dropped the duffel bag on the floor beside the rocking chair. But the playful wink that followed his words told a different story.

She looked away to unzip the bag, then frowned as she rifled through the contents. "Everything is ice-cold."

"The bag was in your car, overnight, in the middle of winter," he pointed out reasonably.

"And, as I discovered yesterday, winter in Montana is a lot different than winter in Texas," she acknowledged, as she pulled out a onesie, a pair of socks and a two-piece outfit. "Can you put these in the clothes dryer for a few minutes?"

He took the items from her hand. "They're not wet."

"No, but they're cold," she said again. "And a quick tumble in the dryer will warm them up to a more comfortable temperature for Cody."

He shrugged but headed out to do her bidding. Or maybe he was grateful for any excuse to leave her with the baby that he didn't believe was his.

Maybe he was right to be skeptical.

Maybe Leighton had been mistaken.

And maybe, after having spent a couple of days with Cody, he understood now how much time and attention a baby needed and would willingly accede to her request to take her nephew back to Dallas.

When Wilder returned with the warm garments, Beth quickly dressed the baby in a red top that had an appliqué reindeer head with Christmas lights looped around its antlers and a pair of dark brown corduroy pants.

"Very festive," Wilder noted.

"He has a lot of holiday outfits," she confided. "Every time I was out shopping, I seemed to find another one that I just couldn't resist."

"And all those Christmas gifts in the back seat of your car—more things you couldn't resist?" he guessed.

"He's my only nephew," she said, by way of explanation. "And it's his first Christmas."

"Do you want me to bring the presents inside?"

She shook her head. "Thanks, but I'd rather celebrate with Cody at home. And since I'm rested now, thanks to you and your kind hospitality, we can be on our way."

Now it was Wilder who shook his head. "I don't think that's a good idea."

"You can't want us to stay here," she said.

"Nothing has been about what I want since Leighton left her baby on my doorstep," he acknowledged.

"And considering what an inconvenience that's obviously been for you, why would you object to us leaving?" she asked coolly.

"Because I still don't know why your sister brought her baby to Rust Creek Falls instead of leaving him in Dallas with you," he said.

"No one but Leighton knows what she was thinking," Beth said.

"Maybe you don't know, but you can probably guess," he suggested.

Beth didn't respond to that. Because yes, she probably could guess. But she had no intention of sharing her suppositions with this man who might or might not be Cody's father and who, in any event, had no right to pry into the painful details of her often difficult relationship with her sister.

A relationship that she'd been certain was turning a corner—before recent events proved otherwise.

"And until you can answer that question to my satisfaction, the baby isn't going anywhere," Wilder said.

An assertion that, of course, put her back up.

"Who put you—a cowboy who clearly doesn't have the first clue about parenting and might not even be Cody's biological father—in charge?" she demanded.

"Your sister," he answered. "When she left her kid with me."

"My sister obviously wasn't thinking clearly," Beth said.

"I don't disagree, but that doesn't change the fact that she brought the baby here."

She hated that he was right. Even more, she hated that Leighton hadn't trusted her enough to talk to her about her plans. Instead, she'd snuck away, leaving only a cryptic note that did nothing to alleviate Beth's worries. And thinking about it now only made her head hurt. She lifted a hand and pressed her fingertips to her temple, as if that might assuage the ache.

"You're probably hungry," Wilder said, his tone more conciliatory than confrontational now.

She frowned. "What?"

"I'm guessing that your head hurts because you haven't eaten," he clarified.

"How do you…oh." She dropped her hand away.

"When did you last have a meal?"

"I grabbed a burger last night when I fueled up my car outside of Bozeman." But she'd only managed to choke down a few bites of the tasteless patty before she'd wrapped it up again and tossed it back into the bag.

"Well, according to the schedule I was given, it's time for the baby to have a bottle, so let's get you something to eat, too," he suggested.

"I'll be down in a minute," she said, reaching for the duffel bag. "I just want to change my clothes first."

"Did you want me to warm yours in the dryer, too?"

Though she didn't relish the idea of wriggling into cold undergarments, it was preferable to handing her bra and panties to a stranger. Especially a sexy stranger who had undoubtedly removed sexier undergarments from her sister's body.

"Thanks, but I'll be fine," she told him.

"Okay, I'll get started fixing the bottle."

She didn't ask him to take Cody and he didn't offer. She did wonder if his reticence was a result of not knowing what to do to take care of a baby or not wanting to acknowledge that Cody might be his.

And she had no intention of pushing him outside of his comfort zone. As far as she was concerned, the sooner he realized that he couldn't handle taking care of an infant, the sooner she could be on her way back to Dallas with her nephew.

When she was changed, she retraced her steps—as best she could recall—from the night before. But it had been dark then, and she'd been focused on Wilder's form moving ahead of her, unable to see much of anything else. In the light of day, she could appreciate the warmth and design of the home that Wilder lived in with…well, she had no idea who else lived in this house. Obviously she had more questions about the man than answers, but hopefully that would change over lunch.

Her stomach growled in support of that plan.

She reached the bottom step and turned—apparently in the wrong direction. Because she found herself in a family room with a grouping of leather furniture around a stone fireplace and a towering Christmas tree that almost touched the vaulted beam ceiling.

"Look at that," she said to Cody, her voice a reverent whisper as she moved closer. "It's almost as big as the tree at the mall where we saw Santa."

Of course, Cody didn't understand what she was talking about and would have no memory of the event even if he did. By the time they'd got to the front of the line and it was his turn to see the jolly man in the red suit, he was fast asleep. Beth hadn't wanted to wake him and risk ending up with a photo of an unhappy or crying baby. Instead, she had a beautiful photo of her nephew, decked out in a red velvet Santa sleeper and matching hat, peacefully tucked into the crook of Santa's arm.

She'd bought two copies of the photo and had framed and wrapped the second one as a Christmas gift for her sister. Of course, she'd invited Leighton to go to the mall with them, but her sister had waved off the suggestion, insisting that Cody was too young to even care. It was undoubtedly true, and yet, Beth couldn't let the occasion of his first Christmas pass without a visit to Santa.

She pushed the memory aside to focus on the tree in

front of her now. It wasn't just big, it was beautifully decorated in what she would call "country chic," with burlap ribbon, handcrafted wooden ornaments, home-sewn felt shapes, crocheted snowflakes, tied clusters of dried fruit, sprigs of berries and striped candy canes.

And unlike the plastic tree in the mall, this one was real. She could smell the rich, fragrant scent of pine in the air.

"Did you get lost?"

She started, turned. "What?"

A smile twitched at the corners of Wilder's mouth, somehow making him look even more unbelievably handsome, and making her wonder what was wrong with her that she could be so immediately and undeniably attracted to the man who might very well be her nephew's father.

"I asked if you got lost," he said.

"Oh, no. I mean, I took a wrong turn, and then..." She shrugged. "I got distracted. You have a beautiful home."

"It's got good bones," he said, turning to exit the room, no doubt expecting her to follow. Which, of course, she did. "But it's also been a lot of work to renovate and update."

"Have you done the work yourself?" she asked, glancing at the framed photos on the sideboard as they passed through the dining room. She was tempted to pause and examine the pictures more closely, but her empty stomach growled to remind her that she had other priorities at the moment.

"Me, my brothers and our dad," he said, handing her a ready-made bottle for the baby.

"Thanks," she said. "But I would have mixed up his formula."

"I just followed the instructions on the label."

She nibbled on her bottom lip, not wanting to appear ungrateful but needing to ask, "Did you use previously boiled water?"

"That's what the instructions said to do," he pointed out. "Plus Hunter, one of my brothers, gave me a crash course on basic childcare."

"He has kids?" Beth guessed, testing the temperature of the formula by shaking a few drops onto the inside of her wrist.

"One. A six-and-a-half-year-old daughter."

"There's no better teacher than experience," Beth said. "But in the absence of experience, there are some good childcare books that help. Leighton had about half a dozen beside her bed when she was pregnant."

She didn't tell him that she'd bought the books for her sister, or admit that Leighton hadn't cracked the covers on most of them. Because her sister had never been a fan of book learning—preferring to figure things out as she went along.

"I have to admit, that surprises me a little," he told her. "The Leighton I knew wasn't really the maternal type."

"I wouldn't have thought so, either," she admitted, as she settled into a chair at the table to give Cody his bottle. "But everything changed when she found out she was pregnant."

Wilder grabbed a mug from the cupboard and filled it from the carafe on a warming burner. "Are you a coffee drinker?" he asked.

"Only on days ending in a 'y,'" she told him.

He chuckled at that as he reached for another mug, then filled it with the steaming brew.

"Cream? Sugar?"

"Cream, please."

He opened the fridge to retrieve the carton, then added a splash to her cup and set it in front of her.

"Thanks." She lifted the mug to her lips and sipped. "That's good and strong."

"It's the only way my dad knows how to make it."

"So this is his house?" she guessed.

Wilder nodded. "When we first moved to Rust Creek Falls, in the summer, Xander and Finn lived here, too. But Xander and Lily have their own place closer to town now, and Finn and Avery renovated a cabin on the far side of the property, so it's just me and my dad left."

"So you've got three brothers?" She wasn't just making conversation; she was genuinely curious to learn more about his family, who might prove to be her nephew's family, too.

"No, I've got five brothers."

"Five?"

He nodded.

"Wow. Six boys. Your mom obviously had her hands full," she remarked.

"Maybe that's why she took off before my first birthday," he noted.

Chapter Four

Beth winced. "I'm sorry."

Wilder immediately waved off her apology. "No reason to be. You couldn't know."

"All the more reason not to speak without thinking." Then, in an apparent effort to smooth over the awkwardness, she quickly changed the subject. "Tell me about your brothers."

He responded readily, happy not to delve any deeper into the details of his mother's abandonment—especially when he honestly didn't know most of them. "Logan, the oldest, is married to Sarah. Hunter's a year younger, the one with the six-and-a-half-year-old daughter, and now engaged to Merry—that's with a capital 'M' followed by an 'e,'" he clarified. "Although I suppose it's also accurate the other way, too.

"Anyway, next after Hunter is Xander, who's married to Lily. Then there's Finn, who's married to Avery and expecting a baby in the spring, and finally Knox, who's married to Gen."

"So all of your brothers are married or engaged," she mused.

He nodded.

"You're not feeling any pressure to follow in their footsteps?"

"Not at all. I'm perfectly happy with my life the way it is," he assured her.

Then his gaze slid in Cody's direction, and when it

shifted back again, the look on Beth's face told him she knew that what he really meant was that he'd been perfectly happy with his life the way it *was*.

He turned to the fridge, away from her knowing expression. "I promised you food," he said. "What are you in the mood for?"

"Oh, um, just some toast would be fine," she said, as she settled into a chair at the table and positioned the bottle close to the baby's mouth. Cody immediately latched onto the nipple and began sucking.

"How about a sandwich?" he suggested.

"That sounds even better," she agreed.

"Do you like turkey?"

"Almost as much as coffee."

He pulled a cellophane-covered platter from the refrigerator.

"That's a lot of turkey," she noted.

"We had a full house for the Christmas meal, so my dad insisted on two birds to ensure we'd have leftover for sandwiches," he explained.

"I'd love a turkey sandwich—if you're sure he wouldn't mind sharing," Beth said.

"There's plenty." He pulled the plastic wrap off the meat. "I guess you didn't get to enjoy Christmas dinner, did you?"

She shook her head. "I mostly fueled myself on coffee and doughnuts."

More coffee than doughnuts, Wilder guessed, with a glance at her thin frame. He generally preferred the women he dated to look like women, with curves rather than angles. Beth was all angles, and yet, there was something about her—an innate warmth and sweetness that appealed to him.

The observation made him frown. Because while he appreciated the female form in various shapes and sizes,

Beth wasn't a female to be ogled—she was Cody's aunt. Leighton's sister.

And definitely not his type.

"White or dark meat?" he asked, turning his attention back to his task.

"Either or," she said. "And I can make my own sandwich."

"You're feeding the baby," he noted. "And that's something I'm not so good at."

"Your brother didn't give you a tutorial?" she teased.

"Apparently I'm not a very quick learner."

Beth smiled at that. "You're lucky your family is so supportive."

"Is 'supportive' another word for 'nosy and interfering?'"

"When it comes to family relationships, there's often some overlap," she acknowledged.

"Is your family supportive?"

"There's just me and Leighton—and Cody—now," she told him. "Our parents were killed during a bank robbery gone wrong almost ten years ago. Innocent bystanders."

Though the words were spoken matter-of-factly, the flatness of her tone suggested that the passage of time had done little to dull the heartache. As someone who'd grown up without a mother, he understood how the pain of loss could linger and wished he could take back the question.

"I'm sorry," he said instead, sounding and feeling awkward.

"Thanks." She eased the nipple of the already empty bottle from the baby's mouth and turned him onto her shoulder, gently rubbing his back.

Was it a maternal instinct that allowed women to anticipate and respond to an infant's needs? Or was it, as his brother had suggested, a parenting instinct? In which case, it was an instinct that Wilder obviously lacked.

"He was hungry," he noted.

"He always is," Beth remarked.

"And so are you," he remembered, refocusing on his task. "Cranberry or mayo?"

"Both."

Wilder made a face but retrieved the condiments from the fridge.

"Coleslaw?" he asked, when he'd cut the sandwiches and set them on two plates.

Her stomach grumbled a response before she did. "Sure."

He spooned some onto the plate beside her sandwich and set it on the table. After Cody had burped, she put him in his car seat and picked up her sandwich.

Wilder expected her to nibble around the crust, pretending more than eating, so he was surprised to see her take a hearty bite. And even more so when she closed her eyes and let out a blissful sigh that he was more accustomed to hearing in the bedroom than the kitchen.

"Oh. My. Goodness." She chewed slowly, swallowed. "You make a really good turkey sandwich."

It wasn't the only thing he did really well. In fact, sandwich-making didn't even crack the top ten list of things he did to please a woman, but he'd be happy to show her—

No. He immediately cut off his wayward thought, unwilling to go there with Beth, who wasn't just a guest under his roof but the baby's aunt.

He cleared his throat along with his mind. "I only assembled the ingredients," he told her. "Lily worked her magic with the bird."

"Lily is…married to Knox?"

He shook his head. "Xander. She runs her own business—Lily's Home Cookin'—now, but she used to be a cook at Maverick Manor."

"What's Maverick Manor?"

"The only decent hotel between here and Kalispell. It was originally an enormous house, nicknamed Bledsoe's Folly in honor of the man who built it. When he died, it stood dark and empty for a lot of years until Nate Crawford bought it and turned it into a hotel."

"A relative of yours?" she guessed.

"Apparently."

"Do you have a lot of family in Rust Creek Falls?" she asked.

"You can't walk down Sawmill Street without bumping into a Crawford—or two or three," he told her. "I thought I'd miss the anonymity of living in a big city, but there's something about this place that makes it feel like home already."

"Maybe the fact that you can't walk down Sawmill Street without bumping into a Crawford," she said, echoing his own words.

He chuckled. "That might be part of it."

She picked up the second half of her sandwich. "I honestly can't remember the last time I had turkey," she told him. "But I'm sure I don't remember it tasting this good."

He popped the last bite of his own sandwich into his mouth. "Last Christmas?"

"What?"

"You said you couldn't remember the last time you had turkey," he reminded her. "I suggested that it was probably last Christmas."

She shook her head. "I cooked a ham. Leighton isn't a fan of turkey."

"Do you always cater to your sister's preferences?"

"Not always," she denied. "But I probably do give in to her more often than I should."

"And I'll bet the more you indulge her, the more she takes advantage."

Beth frowned at his blunt assessment, but she didn't contradict it.

Aware that he was edging toward sensitive territory, he shifted the topic of conversation again. "Do you want anything else to eat?"

She shook her head as she pushed her now empty plate aside. "No, that was more than enough, thanks."

"Are you sure? Because I'm going to have a piece of leftover apple pie."

"I'm sure," she said. "Although if you'd said pumpkin, I might have been tempted."

"We have that, too," he told her. "And bourbon whipped cream."

"You're the devil, aren't you?"

"'A handsome devil' is what the ladies usually say," he replied, with a flirtatious wink.

Beth didn't respond to Wilder's comment, not even with a hint of a smile. If anything, she looked...disapproving.

Well, perhaps his teasing remark hadn't been entirely appropriate considering that she was the sister of one of his former lovers who believed that he was the father of her nephew.

"Was that a 'yes' to the bourbon whipped cream?" he asked, as he plated a slice of pumpkin pie.

"That was a 'yes, please,'" she confirmed, rising from the table to retrieve the coffee carafe from the warmer.

He opened the lid of the container and scooped a generous spoonful of the creamy topping onto the pie. Then he cut a wedge of apple for himself, grabbed two forks from the drawer and carried the plates and cutlery to the table.

"Thanks," she said, topping up his mug with coffee before refilling her own.

He nodded and straddled the seat across from her.

"Are you older or younger than Leighton?" he asked, when she sat down again.

"Older, by twenty-two months," she said, picking up her fork.

His lips curved as he popped the first bite of pie into his mouth.

"What?" she asked, though he hadn't spoken a single word.

"Just the way you said 'twenty-two months,'" he remarked. "I'll bet you held that over her head when you were growing up together."

"I did not," she immediately denied, dipping her fork into her pie.

"Yes, you did," he said. "As the older sibling, you probably couldn't help yourself. I know my brothers always held their maturity over me."

She seemed to consider this comment as she chewed, then slowly nodded. "Maybe I did," she acknowledged. "Of course, that completely backfired on me a few years ago, after my twenty-fifth birthday, when she started to take pleasure in pointing out that she was twenty-two months younger."

He chuckled. "Just like I refer to my brothers as 'old men' now. 'Old' *and* 'married' if I'm talking about Logan, Finn, Xander or Knox—because that's two nails in the coffin."

She frowned at that. "Not everyone looks at marriage as a death sentence."

"It was a joke," he told her.

"Was it?" she countered.

"You know, now that I've had some time to think about it, I do recall Leighton mentioning a sister…and referring to her as a stick-in-the-mud."

"That would be me," Beth agreed.

Now *he* frowned. "It's no fun to take a shot at someone who doesn't shoot back."

"Why would you expect anything different from a stick-in-the-mud?" she asked him. "And, for the record, she's also referred to me as a worrywart, a spoilsport and a killjoy."

"And the one who always does the right thing," he added.

"What?"

"I forgot that," he said, speaking almost to himself. "I guess she talked about you more than I realized, because I can remember her telling me that you were the one who always did the right thing. 'Little Miss Perfect'—cleaning up the messes she made."

"Not a term of endearment," she acknowledged wryly.

"I'm not so sure," he mused. "I think she really looks up to you, her older-by-twenty-two-months sister."

That earned him a hint of a smile. And he couldn't help noticing how pretty she was when she smiled.

But apparently she'd said everything she intended to on the subject of her sister, because the next time Beth spoke, it was to ask a completely random question.

"Aren't you supposed to be ranching?"

The vagueness and broadness of the question proved to Wilder that she was as unfamiliar with the responsibilities of a rancher as he was those of a parent.

"I wish," he said.

At her lifted brow, he shrugged. "Although ranching is a year-round job, things slow down a little in winter. Aside from feeding the cattle and livestock every day, we mostly focus on maintenance of buildings and equipment and perimeter fence checks, cutting and collecting firewood, and clearing snow."

"That sounds busy enough to me," she remarked.

"It is," he agreed. "But my dad assured me that he had plenty of hands to do the chores that needed to be done and that my hands should be taking care of the baby."

"Obviously he hasn't seen you try to change a diaper," she teased.

"Kids aren't really my thing," he acknowledged. Not that there was any chance she might have assumed otherwise.

"You know there's an easy way out of your dilemma," she said. "You could let me take Cody back to Dallas and pretend the last forty-eight hours never happened."

"Don't think I'm not tempted, but I don't walk away from my mistakes."

Beth bristled. "Cody is *not* a mistake."

"I didn't mean that the way it sounded," he said, immediately regretting his unthinking response.

"Then what did you mean?" she challenged.

"Let me just say that I wasn't thrilled to learn that I might be a father to a baby I didn't know anything about," Wilder told her. "And your questions about his paternity make me wonder how many other men Leighton was dating while we were together."

"I don't know," Beth admitted. "She didn't share those kinds of details with me."

Except to point out that Leighton, unlike Beth, had a personal life. Or remark that Beth was such a killjoy no one would ever be interested in her.

Beth never let her sister know how much those comments hurt. Because as much as Leighton could be kind and generous at times, she could also be hard and cruel, and—like a shark scenting blood—any sign of weakness could escalate her attack.

Beth pushed those uncomfortable memories aside to refocus on her conversation with Wilder. "And I didn't mean to suggest that there were others…during the time that she was with you. She didn't juggle men like that."

"That's a relief, I guess," he noted.

But the glance he sent in the direction of the now sleeping baby suggested to Beth that he was still more wary than reassured.

"My dad seems convinced that he's a Crawford, but I'm not quite willing to let myself be put on the hook on the basis of his gut feeling."

"If that's your attitude, then I really hope you're not Cody's father," she said.

"You don't think I should want proof?"

"Of course you should want proof," she said. "But instead of worrying about whether you're 'on the hook,' you might consider fatherhood as an opportunity rather than an obligation."

"I guess there's only one way to decide our next step," he said, and reached for his cell phone.

"Who are you calling?" Beth asked, as she dipped her fork into her pie again.

"The medical clinic—as soon as I can find the number," he said, searching for the listing.

"For a paternity test?" she guessed.

He nodded.

She chewed as Wilder connected the call, but her attention was no longer on the pie.

"Okay," Wilder said, when he'd set his phone aside again. "We've got an appointment at eleven o'clock tomorrow morning."

"That was quick," she said, surprised.

"The sooner we get the test done, the sooner we can get the results," he pointed out.

She nodded her agreement, eager to know the truth and still a little bit worried about what that truth might be.

"If it turns out that the baby isn't mine, I won't object to you taking him back to Dallas," Wilder continued. "Until then, however, he isn't going anywhere."

"But…the results will probably take several days. Maybe even longer."

"I guess that's possible," he acknowledged.

"You can't expect me to stay in Rust Creek Falls that long," she protested.

"You can leave anytime you want," he said. "But you'll leave without the baby."

Chapter Five

Wilder could tell his statement had surprised her. It had surprised him, too. If Beth had shown up immediately after Leighton had left the baby on his doorstep, he would have happily turned the infant over to his aunt. But somehow, over the past forty-eight hours, he'd started to get attached to the little guy.

He wasn't quite ready to accept that the kid was his, and truthfully—for Cody's sake—he still hoped Leighton had been wrong in identifying him as the dad. But he was invested in discovering the truth now, and determined to have it before making any decisions about his future.

"But my job is in Dallas," Beth protested. "My *life* is in Dallas."

"What is your job?" Wilder asked.

"I teach kindergarten."

"Then it's your winter break right now, isn't it?" he pointed out logically.

"It is," she acknowledged. "And I didn't plan on spending my holidays in Montana."

He shrugged. "As I said, you can go anytime you want."

"But you won't let me take Cody with me."

"Nope," he confirmed.

She sighed. "Is there a hotel in town?"

"Only Maverick Manor, just off the highway. But it's booked through to the New Year."

"Motel, then? Or bed-and-breakfast?"

"There's Strickland's Boarding House in town," he told

her. "But if you plan on staying in Rust Creek Falls, there's no reason you can't stay here. The room you slept in last night has been empty since Finn moved out."

"Are you sure the rest of your family wouldn't mind?"

"It's just me and my dad here now," he said. "And truthfully, I wouldn't object to some help with the baby."

"Cody," she said.

He scowled. "What?"

"His name is Cody."

"I know his name."

"Do you? Because I haven't heard you say it—not even once."

His scowl deepened at that.

"It's only four letters. Just two short syllables. *Co-dy*," she said again, deliberately emphasizing each syllable.

"I know his name," Wilder repeated.

"But you won't get attached if you don't use it," she guessed. "If you continue to refer to him as 'the baby,' and it turns out that he's not *your* baby, it'll be easier for you to walk away."

Annoyed by her insightful assessment—though not necessarily willing to believe it was true—he hit back. "I think I'm beginning to see why Leighton brought her baby here rather than leaving him with you."

Surprise and hurt were clearly reflected in her eyes before she sucked in a breath and quickly looked away.

Wilder winced. "I'm sorry."

"Are you?" she challenged, her eyes shiny with what he suspected were tears.

"I sometimes lash out when I'm feeling defensive, and you got caught in the crossfire," he explained.

"And I can be overprotective of those I love," she said. "I want what's best for Cody, and apparently Leighton thought that was you, so you need to step up and act like his father."

"*If* I am his father," Wilder said, still not quite ready to believe it was possible.

Because in the brief time that he'd been with Leighton, there'd been no forgotten or broken condoms, no reason at all for him to suspect she might have been pregnant with his child when they parted ways.

Yet somehow, in the short time that the baby—*Cody,* he mentally amended—had been at the ranch, Wilder had started to accept that fatherhood might not be the worst thing that could happen to him. That maybe it was time for him to not just step up but grow up.

Beth nodded in acknowledgement of his point as a knock sounded.

Before he could get up to answer the summons, the door opened and Avery stepped inside, kicking snow off her boots.

"No babies on your doorstep today?" his sister-in-law teased in lieu of a greeting.

"No," he said. "And not funny."

"I don't know," Beth said, maybe trying to prove that she wasn't a complete stick-in-the-mud. "I thought it was pretty funny."

Avery grinned. "That's because you have a better sense of humor than my grumpy brother-in-law."

"I have reason to be grumpy," he told her. "I was up I-don't-know-how-many times in the night with the baby."

His brother's wife was immediately sympathetic. "I'm not surprised the little guy had a restless night, in an unfamiliar place with people he doesn't know."

"And, as a result of his restless night, *I* had a restless night," Wilder felt compelled to point out.

"Actually, that's why I stopped by," she said. "To see if you were managing okay with the baby. I wished we could have stayed later the other night, but we had to get back to Pumpkin."

"Pumpkin is a goat," Wilder explained to Beth.

"Goat?" she echoed, as if uncertain she'd heard him correctly.

"Don't ask," he warned. "Because if you do, she'll never stop talking about it."

Avery's narrowed gaze promised retribution for what she perceived as the slight of her beloved pet, but she refocused on the purpose of her visit to ask again, "So how are you managing with Cody?"

"Lucky for the kid, I've got some help now," he said.

His sister-in-law's attention shifted back to Beth. "You must be the owner of the car in the driveway with the Texas plates."

She nodded and offered her hand. "Beth Ames. I'm Cody's aunt."

"It's nice to meet you. I'm Avery, one of Wilder's sisters-in-law," she introduced herself. "And since I'm obviously not needed here, I'm going to head back to my place. The furniture for the nursery was delivered this morning, and I can't wait to get it set up."

"You mean you can't wait to nag Finn to set it up," Wilder said firmly, concerned that his sister-in-law might attempt to tackle the chore on her own.

"Finn's busy trying to rebuild the engine of some piece of equipment."

"The baler?" Wilder suggested.

"Maybe. I sometimes tune out when he's grumbling about stuff like that," she admitted. "And anyway, the point is that I know my way around a toolbox well enough to put the furniture together."

"You should wait for Finn to do it," Wilder insisted.

"I don't want to wait," Avery told him.

He sighed. "Fine. If Beth doesn't mind me leaving Cody in her capable hands, I'll go put your furniture together."

"Of course I don't mind taking care of *my nephew*," she said pointedly.

"And I'd be happy to keep Beth company while you're gone," Avery said.

"Why does that *not* reassure me?" he wondered aloud.

His sister-in-law grinned. "I won't spill all of your deepest, darkest secrets," she promised. "But only because I don't know them all."

"Lucky me," he said dryly.

"But Finn has shared enough stories that I can probably keep Beth entertained until you're back."

"I'm glad you stopped by," Beth said to Avery when Wilder had gone. "Because I wanted to thank you personally for helping take care of Cody. Wilder said you've been a big help."

"It was my pleasure," Avery said. "Your nephew is a real sweetie."

"I think so," she agreed, with a smile.

"Plus—" Avery rubbed a hand over her rounded belly "—it was good practice for my own little bundle of joy."

"Wilder said you're due in the spring?"

"Early March," the other woman confirmed. "I feel as if I've been pregnant forever, but now I can finally almost see the light at the end of the tunnel." Then she sighed. "What I can't see are my feet. But maybe that's a good thing, because I haven't had a pedicure in...forever."

"You should treat yourself," Beth said. "Because you'll have even less time for those kinds of indulgences once your baby comes."

"I'd love to treat myself," Avery agreed. "Unfortunately, there isn't a spa in Rust Creek Falls. It's one of the things I miss about living in Dallas."

"You're from Texas, too?"

"Born and raised," the expectant mom confirmed.

"So what brought you to Montana?"

"Finn," she said. "We'd known each other in Dallas, and when I heard he'd moved to Rust Creek Falls, I came here to see him and decided to stay."

"You know it's love when," Beth said.

Avery chuckled. "Yeah, it was a pretty big change," she acknowledged. "But Rust Creek Falls isn't so bad, once you get used to it."

"I don't plan on being here long enough to get used to it," Beth said.

"That's too bad. Because Wilder's going to need some help learning how to be a dad to Cody."

"Do you really think he's interested in being a dad?" she asked dubiously.

"I *know* he is," Avery said. "Even if *he* doesn't know it yet."

Beth frowned at that.

"He just needs some time to get used to the idea, especially considering how the happy news was delivered."

"I encouraged Leighton to get in touch with the father, as soon as she told me she was pregnant, but she insisted he wouldn't want to know," Beth confided.

"I'm not judging your sister," the other woman hastened to assure her. "I walked more than a few miles in her shoes."

Beth's confusion must have shown on her face, because Avery said, "You didn't know that I was pregnant with Finn's baby before we got married?"

She shook her head.

"Well, I was," Avery said. "And although I came to Rust Creek Falls specifically to tell him that we were going to have a baby, it still took me a long time to find the right words—or any words, really."

"But you did it," Beth noted.

"I did it," the other woman confirmed. "And then, as if I

wasn't freaked out enough about being pregnant, I freaked out even more when Finn suggested we get married."

"You didn't want to get married?"

"I didn't know what I wanted. I was scared and confused and everything just seemed to be happening so fast. We had a one-night stand, I got pregnant, I told him about the baby, he proposed, we got married—" she paused then, a smile curving her lips "—and then we fell in love."

Beth sighed, a little wistfully. "It sounds like a romance novel."

Avery chuckled. "There was enough drama between our families to fill a lot of pages, that's for sure."

"And now you're one big happy family."

"Or faking it," Avery said. "But I don't care if our respective fathers are just going through the motions, because I know that Finn loves me as much as I love him."

"I'm glad things worked out for you."

Avery rubbed her belly again. "Me, too."

And maybe Beth was guilty of reading too many fairy tales to her kindergarten class, but one of the reasons she'd continued to encourage—Leighton would probably say "nag"—her sister to reach out to Cody's father was that she wanted a happy ending for them, too.

Though leaving the baby at his door wasn't quite what she'd had in mind, Beth wanted to believe it was the first step toward a possible reconciliation of Cody's parents.

Assuming that Wilder was the little boy's father.

Of course, she had no reason to doubt the claim in her sister's letter. No reason except Leighton's confession that she wasn't 100 percent certain.

But if she was being honest, she'd suspected, even at the time, that her sister had only been pretending to be uncertain so that Beth would stop nagging. Because she couldn't be expected to contact the father if she wasn't sure who was the father. And the fact that Leighton had brought Cody here proved she wasn't uncertain at all.

But if Beth acknowledged that the hunky cowboy was her nephew's father, and if Wilder was willing to step up and be his father, where would that leave her?

On her way back to Dallas, alone.

And that scenario wasn't one she wanted to contemplate.

When Avery had gone, Beth took Cody into the family room with the giant Christmas tree for some playtime. The ranch house was so warm and homey, she'd been taken aback to learn that Max was an unmarried rancher with six sons.

Of course, it was possible that he'd had the house professionally furnished. Or maybe one or more of his daughters-in-law had helped with the finishing touches. In any event, Beth felt comfortable in the house, despite being an uninvited guest.

She sat Cody in her lap on the floor and played patty-cake with him, then she entertained him with "Itsy Bitsy Spider" and used his favorite blanket as a curtain for peekaboo.

As much as she always enjoyed playful interaction with her nephew, she understood the importance of alone time, too, to teach him independence. But considering that Cody hadn't seen his mother since Christmas Day, she opted to focus on play today so he wouldn't worry that she'd left him, too.

"How about some tummy time?" she suggested, spreading his blanket out on the carpet.

"This is supposed to help you build strength for sitting up and rolling over," she said, laying him down on his belly on top of the blanket.

Then she stretched out on the carpet facing him, her chin propped up on her folded arms.

Cody lifted his head to look at her, a wide, toothless smile spreading across his face.

"You're already such a strong boy, aren't you?" she said, wiping his drooly chin with the corner of the blanket. "You're going to be rolling over before we know it, then I won't be able to put you down for fear of losing you."

Cody pushed himself up higher, as if to prove he was ready to move on to bigger and better things.

"I lost track of the number of times I had to tell my kids to get their feet off the furniture," a deep voice said from behind her. "But I never objected to anyone sitting on it."

Embarrassed to have been caught in such an undignified position, Beth immediately rolled over and rose to her feet. If his reference to "kids" hadn't already identified him as Wilder's father, she would have guessed the relationship just from looking at him.

She gauged him to be in his midsixties. His handsome face, deeply tanned and lined, attesting to a life spent outdoors. Though she knew him to be a rancher and he was dressed in the cattleman's usual uniform of jeans and plaid shirt, his clothes looked more Rodeo Drive than rodeo.

"Um, hi," she said, scooping Cody up off the floor. "We were just having some tummy time."

He nodded. "I heard."

"Oh." Her cheeks flushed hotter as she wondered how long he'd been standing there, watching them, and if she'd said anything she shouldn't have. She tended to think out loud when she was with Cody, to help build his listening and vocabulary skills, and often didn't even realize she was doing it.

"To build strength for sitting up and rolling over," he noted.

She nodded. "It also reduces the risk of developing a flat spot on the back of the head as a result of spending too much time on his back."

"We didn't worry about that when my boys were babies," Max told her. "Because the conventional wisdom of the time was to put babies to sleep on their tummies."

"Now 'back to sleep' is the recommendation," Beth said.

"I learned that when my first granddaughter was born," he acknowledged. "She's six and a half now—and a total princess."

"Is this hers?" Beth asked, reaching under the sofa to retrieve the Princess Aurora doll she'd spotted earlier.

"It is," Max confirmed. "Hunter called last night, asking me to look for it, and I insisted it wasn't here. Obviously I was wrong."

She gave him the doll. "A fringe benefit of tummy time is finding things you didn't even know you'd lost."

"Well, Wren will certainly be happy that it was found."

"By the way, I'm Beth," she said.

"I guessed as much," he said. "Wilder said you arrived late last night."

Beth nodded. "I'm sorry for showing up unannounced and uninvited," she said. "When Wilder called and said that Cody was here, all I could think about was getting to him."

"You don't need to apologize for caring about your nephew," Max told her. "The kind of love and devotion that compelled you to drive straight through from Dallas is admirable."

"I'd do anything for Cody," she said sincerely.

"But you don't know why his mother left him here with his father?"

She frowned at his ready acceptance of the paternity claim. "You believe Wilder is Cody's dad?"

"Don't you?" he countered.

"I don't know what to believe," she confided.

"Well, having raised six sons of my own, I have no doubt that little boy is a Crawford."

"I'm afraid I'm going to need something a little more scientific than that to be convinced," she told him.

His lips twitched, as if he was fighting a smile. "You're a skeptic, are you?"

"I'd say cautious."

"Is that why you're not married with a family yet?" Max asked.

She was taken aback by both his assumption and the personal nature of the question. "How do you know I'm not?"

"You left Texas on Christmas Day to drive halfway across the country for your sister's son. That suggests to me that you weren't celebrating with your own family."

A valid point, she acknowledged. "I guess I'm still waiting to meet the right person," she said. "And anyway, my focus right now is on Cody—and finding my sister."

"You don't have any idea where she might have gone?"

"I had no idea even that she was coming here," Beth confided.

"You're not close."

It was more a statement than a question, but she responded anyway.

"Not as close as I'd like us to be," she acknowledged, and wondered why she felt guilty for something that wasn't her fault. Or at least not entirely her fault.

But she'd only just met this man and had no intention of opening up her heart—or family history—to him. She definitely wasn't going to say anything that might cause him to view her sister in a negative light. Of course, Leighton's abandonment of her child on his doorstep had likely taken care of that already.

"I had six kids," Max said again. "You don't need to tell me about sibling relationships."

"But we've grown closer since she told me she was

pregnant with Cody. And especially in the past four and a half months."

"And yet she still left Dallas without telling you where she was going," he noted.

She nodded, because yeah, there was no denying that. And no pretending that it didn't hurt.

"Well, you're here now," Max said. "And it's obvious that your nephew is happy to see you, so can I assume you're planning to stay a while?"

"It's looking that way at the moment," she acknowledged. "I offered to go to the boarding house in town, but Wilder was kind enough to invite me to stay here. Assuming it's okay with you."

Max's lips twitched, as if he was fighting a smile. "I'm not sure it was kindness that motivated his offer. But we have plenty of space," he confirmed, before Beth could question his first statement. "And you're welcome to stay as long as you need to."

"I appreciate it," she said. "But if I'm going to stay, I'd like to help out in some way."

"That isn't necessary," Max said.

"I'm not a bad cook," she told him.

The rancher tilted his head, considering her offer. "Do you by any chance know how to make meatloaf?" he asked, with a twinkle in his eye.

"I've got my mother's recipe stored right here," she said, tapping a finger to her head. "And it's the best I've ever tasted."

"In that case, there's a package of ground beef in the fridge."

She smiled, grateful for the opportunity to repay him in some small way for his hospitality. "What time do you like to eat?"

Chapter Six

Wilder felt a little guilty about abandoning the baby in Beth's care while he went to his brother's cabin to put together the nursery furniture. A little guilty and a lot grateful, because the more time he spent with Cody, the more doubts he had that he'd ever figure out this daddy stuff.

He'd been making a sincere effort, but he didn't seem to have any kind of instincts when it came to interpreting the baby's needs. Logan claimed he could tell if Sophia was hungry or wet or tired by the sound of her cry. Wilder only wanted to stop the baby from crying, but his attempts weren't always successful.

He had made some progress, though. The baby had only peed on Wilder once. And he was getting pretty good at mixing formula and giving the baby a bottle. But feeding him cereal? He'd swear the kid spit out more than he took in. And when that stuff dried, it was like trying to wash off hardened cement.

Despite his incompetence and missteps, Cody was a pretty good sport about everything. And just last night—in the middle of the night, when he'd been summoned by the baby's cries and tried to rock him back to sleep, the little guy had stared at him for a long time and then, finally, he'd smiled at him.

And Wilder's heart had completely melted.

The reaction had both surprised and unnerved him. Because while he'd figured he would probably become a dad one day, that day was supposed to be in the distant future. So far down the road he couldn't even see a speck of it on the horizon. It wasn't supposed to be now. And it definitely wasn't supposed to happen without any warning or preparation.

So maybe he took his time with the furniture, checking and double-checking that every bolt and screw was securely fastened. Then he moved it into position in the room—or at least as he thought it should be positioned—and tidied up all the packaging. Only when he'd run out of tasks and couldn't imagine any more, did he leave his brother's cabin to return to the main house.

He hung his coat up on a hook inside the door, beside Beth's. Because of course she was still there—where would she have gone while he was out?

And even if she did want to go out, she shouldn't venture far in the lightweight coat and useless boots she'd brought from Dallas. If she planned to stay in Rust Creek Falls for any length of time—and apparently she did—she was going to need some proper winter clothing.

He wandered through the house until he found her, sitting in the rocking chair beside the crib, watching Cody sleep. He paused there for a moment, wondering why the image of woman and child suddenly seemed so appealing to him—and maybe wishing the smart and sexy woman wasn't completely off-limits to him.

"Why are you hiding up here?" he asked. Then, as a thought occurred to him, "Did my father scare you off?"

"I'm not hiding," she denied. "And your father isn't scary. A little opinionated and outspoken, perhaps, but not scary."

"So you did meet him?"

She nodded. "We had a brief but pleasant chat."

"Do you have any idea where he is now?"

"I think he went to… Hunter's house?"

"Are you telling me or asking me?"

"Which one of your brothers has the little girl who likes princesses?"

"Hunter," he confirmed.

She nodded. "Then I'm telling you. He went to Hunter's house to return the doll that Wren left here at Christmas."

"And if my father's not home, why are you hiding up here?"

"I'm not hiding," she said again. "I just wanted to be close when Cody wakes up."

"Trust me, you don't need to be close to hear him," Wilder said.

"I didn't hear him during the night," she noted, but rose from the chair to follow him out of the room now.

"Yeah, you were pretty dead to the world when you crashed."

She frowned. "How do you know?"

"Because I walked by the door and saw you passed out on top of the covers."

Apparently she didn't want to venture any further down that path, because she asked instead, "Did you get the crib put together for your sister-in-law?"

"The crib *and* the changing table *and* two dressers." He shook his head. "I don't have enough clothes to fill two dressers. I can't imagine an infant's going to need all that space."

"Your brother and sister-in-law are obviously excited about their first baby."

"You mean their first human baby," he remarked. "Because Avery babies that goat like it *is* a baby."

"They really do have a pet goat?"

"I would not make that up," he assured her.

"Do they keep it in the house?"

"No," he said. "And don't give Avery any ideas, or she'll be after Finn to build another addition."

"Or sweet-talk her brother-in-law into doing it," Beth remarked, tongue in cheek.

"You think she sweet-talked me into putting her furniture together?" he asked, reaching into the cupboard for a mug.

She lifted one slender shoulder in a half shrug, and he couldn't help but notice how her breast rose and fell with the motion.

Off-limits, he reminded himself.

"All I know is Avery got to hang out here with me and then go home to a nursery full of baby furniture without breaking a sweat," Beth said.

"She's almost seven months pregnant. She shouldn't be breaking a sweat," he said, reaching for the coffeepot.

"Are you really going to drink that?" Beth asked, as he filled his mug.

"What else would I do with it?"

"It's been on the warmer for hours. Let me make a fresh pot."

"It's fine," he said, and lifted the mug to his mouth to prove it.

Okay, it was a little stale and slightly burnt, but the hot liquid warmed his body and the caffeine jolted his brain, and that was what mattered. Or maybe it was the interaction with Cody's aunt that revved up his system.

Beth shuddered as she watched him swallow another mouthful.

"I'm guessing you don't want any?"

She shook her head. "I'm coffeed out."

"There are tea bags around here somewhere, if you prefer that. Or juice and soda in the fridge, if you want something cold."

"No, I'm fine, thanks."

He swallowed another mouthful of coffee, then lifted his head and sniffed the air. "What do I smell?"

"Burnt coffee?" she guessed.

"No. Something smells good."

"Oh, your dad wanted meatloaf for dinner."

He opened the oven door to peer inside.

"You're letting the heat out," Beth admonished.

He closed the door. "My dad wanted meatloaf?"

"Why do you sound surprised?"

"Because meatloaf isn't his favorite meal," Wilder admitted.

But it was one of Wilder's favorites, a fact of which his father was well aware. And the fact that Max had asked Beth to prepare one of Wilder's favorite meals started his internal alarms clanging.

Was it possible that his father was attempting to make a match between his youngest son and Cody's aunt? Would he dare?

Of course, the answer to both those questions was "yes." With Max, anything was possible, and he would dare almost anything.

It was also possible that Wilder was being a little bit paranoid.

Except that it wasn't paranoia if it was true, and there was no doubt that Max was on a quest to see each of his sons happily married—or that he would never be satisfied with five out of six.

"So...you know how to cook," he mused, remembering that Leighton had claimed she couldn't boil water without a recipe.

"I'm not a gourmet chef, but my mom taught me the basics."

"She taught you but not your sister?"

Beth shrugged. "Leighton wasn't interested in learning."

"Or maybe she was happier to let other people take care of her."

"That's a possibility," Beth acknowledged. "Although

not one that reflects favorably upon the woman who might be the mother of your child."

"I liked your sister well enough, but I wasn't blind to her ability to manipulate people."

"I didn't think you knew her for very long—or very well."

"The Leighton I knew wasn't big on subtlety."

"Fair enough," she decided.

He sensed that Beth, though aware of her sister's faults, would defend Leighton against anyone else's criticism, and decided to shift the focus of their conversation. "I'm curious to know how two sisters, born of the same parents, could grow up to be so different," he told her.

"You have five brothers," she noted. "Are you all cut from the same cloth?"

"Of course not," he acknowledged. "But we all share similar traits—one of which is that women find us irresistible."

Beth rolled her eyes at that.

Most women, he mentally amended.

"Leighton and I share similar traits, too," she said. "Although she was labeled 'the pretty one' and I was 'the smart one,' she's just as smart as me—maybe even smarter."

Wilder had some doubts about that. Not because he questioned Leighton's intelligence, but because Beth was pretty, too. Maybe she didn't play up her attributes the way her sister had done, but her unenhanced beauty was even more alluring because there was no doubt she was real.

"And I think that was part of the problem," Beth continued, drawing his focus back to their conversation. "No one knew she struggled to read because she so quickly memorized the books she was being tested on. She was also good at mental math, so when she transposed numbers on tests, her teachers accused her of not paying attention to what she was doing. It wasn't until she was in high school that her dyslexia was discovered."

"Better late than never," he said.

"You'd think," Beth agreed. "But Leighton balked at being labeled. She wasn't interested in strategies to deal with her learning disability—she preferred to pretend she didn't care."

"Maybe she wasn't pretending," he suggested.

She frowned, as if that was a possibility she'd never considered. "Anyway, I suspect one of the reasons she never learned to cook is that she works at a bar in a restaurant and eats there most of the time."

"Well, I'm definitely glad you learned to cook, because that meatloaf smells really good," he told her, his mouth already watering.

In fact, he was starting to understand how a man could get used to coming in from a hard day's work on the ranch to a homecooked meal every night. Especially if that hot meal was prepared by a hot wife.

Wait! Where the heck had *that* come from?

He frowned at the dregs left in the bottom of his mug, as if the stale coffee was somehow responsible for the wayward idea. Yeah, a lot of things seemed to be changing in his life, but his readiness to put his neck in the marriage noose was *not* one of them.

Pushing the uneasy thought aside, he asked Beth: "So when do we get to eat it?"

They ate forty-five minutes later.

And it *was* good.

If Beth had any doubts about that, they were assuaged when both Wilder and his father refilled their plates. Max even insisted that the men would do the dishes to show their appreciation for "the delicious meal." Of course, Beth had already washed up all the bowls and equipment she'd used in the prep process, so they really only had to put the plates, cutlery and empty baking pan in the dishwasher. Still she was pleased to note that, despite his apparent wealth and status, the Crawford patriarch didn't expect to be waited on hand and foot.

When the men had finished cleaning up, Max headed into town to meet another rancher at the Ace in the Hole for a beer and a discussion about the potential sale of a piece of equipment, leaving Beth alone with Wilder and Cody.

"I forgot to ask earlier—do you have a bathtub?" She posed the question to Wilder after his father had gone.

"You want to take a bath?"

"Not for me," she said. "For Cody."

"There's one in my dad's bathroom," he told her.

"Do you think he'd mind if we used it?"

"Of course not."

"Great," she said. "If you can grab a couple of towels and a washcloth, I'll get Cody's baby shampoo and bodywash."

He went to get the requested towels while she retrieved the toiletries. Wilder had pointed out the door to Max's room earlier, but despite his assurance that his father wouldn't mind her making use of his en suite bath, she still hesitated to enter the Crawford patriarch's personal space.

"You can knock, if you want," he teased, when he found her hovering outside his father's room. "But he's not home, so he won't answer."

"I know," she admitted. "But it seems like a violation of his privacy to just walk right in."

"I'll go first," he said. "And kick aside any clothes he's left on the floor."

She followed in his wake, trying not to be too nosy but unable to resist a quick peek at Max's inner sanctum—which was furnished in a simple and masculine style and neat as a pin.

"You knew there wouldn't be any clothes lying around, didn't you?"

"Yeah," he admitted, leading the way to the en suite bath. "My dad has never tolerated messiness or clutter—which is inevitable with six kids under one roof. Not even the full-time housekeeper we had in Dallas could keep up with us."

"I can't imagine any one woman being able to keep up with six kids," she said sincerely. "But kudos to her for trying."

He grinned at that and hit the light switch on the wall, illuminating a bathroom that was half the size of the enormous bedroom and twice as luxurious.

"Wow," she said softly, grateful that he seemed to assume she was reacting to the revelation of the facilities rather than the curve of his lips.

"My dad spared no expense in here," he confirmed. "But his two priorities were a shower with body jets and a tub big enough for his horse."

She stared down at the oversize soaker tub and imagined sinking into steamy water filled with mountains of bubbles. Of course, the tub was more than big enough for two, and her traitorous imagination immediately invited Wilder's big, hard body to join her—

She blinked and quickly dispelled the tantalizing image.

"I wouldn't be surprised if you could get a horse in there," she agreed, not looking at him. "Because it's definitely too big for a baby."

"So what are you going to do?" he asked.

Since turning her bubble bath fantasy into a reality wasn't ever going to happen, she suggested, "Plan B."

"I thought you were joking when you said the kitchen sink," Wilder admitted.

Beth shook her head as she put the stopper in and

turned on the faucet, testing the water temperature with the inside of her wrist. When there was about six inches of water, she took one of the folded towels and set it in the bottom of the sink.

"I thought the towels were for drying the baby."

"The second towel is for drying the baby," she said. "This one is so he doesn't slip."

"Why do I think you've done this before?"

"Because I have." She rolled up the sleeves of her shirt. "One weekend when Cody stayed with me, I forgot to pack his baby tub along with the rest of his things, so…Plan B."

"*You* forgot to pack his tub?"

"That's what I said." She stripped the baby down to his diaper, then tested the temperature of the water again with her elbow before removing that final barrier and easing the little guy into the water.

"His mom didn't pack his stuff?" Wilder asked.

"Sometimes," Beth said.

It was a surprisingly vague response from a woman who usually seemed happy to talk about her nephew—and extol Leighton's maternal virtues. And though Wilder was tempted to press for more details, or at least inquire as to how many weekends she'd looked after a baby who was only four months old, he decided to let the topic slide—at least for now.

"What do you need me to do?" he asked instead.

"Why don't you wash him while I hold him?" she suggested.

"Because washing seems a lot more complicated than holding," he replied honestly.

She smiled but didn't offer to reassign tasks.

Of course, she was already up to her elbows in the water, holding the baby upright so he didn't topple over.

"Wet the washcloth, wring out the excess water and

gently clean his face and neck. And don't forget behind his ears," she said.

He followed her directions, feeling awkward and inept—and far too aware of the scent of his shampoo in her hair as he huddled close to her by the sink.

"Now squeeze a drop of bodywash onto the cloth and work up a lather," she said.

She patiently talked him through the process of washing and rinsing the baby's body, then his hair, while she held Cody in place.

"This will be a lot easier once he's able to sit up on his own," she promised.

"And a lot easier with help," he acknowledged. "I don't think I could have tackled this on my own."

"Sponge baths work in a pinch," she said. "But it's good to get babies accustomed to the water, and Cody always seems to enjoy his bath."

It was obvious to Wilder that she'd performed the same task dozens of times before, and he was grateful for her help and guidance. But her obvious ease with and affection for her nephew caused him to question again why Leighton, wanting a break from the demands of parenthood, hadn't chosen to leave the baby with Beth.

While he was mulling over these questions, she'd toweled off, diapered and dressed the baby.

"There's my sweet-smelling boy," she said, nuzzling him for a moment before setting him in his car seat.

"Only until he fills his diaper again," Wilder noted.

Beth shook her head as she turned back to the sink to drain the water.

It was then Wilder noticed that the front of her shirt was wet—and plastered against her like a second skin.

Though he knew he shouldn't stare, he couldn't tear his gaze away from the delicate lace pattern of her bra, clearly visible through the now-transparent fabric, and he couldn't help but admire the nicely rounded shape of the breasts inside the lace cups.

She lifted the sodden towel from the sink and twisted it in her hands to squeeze out the excess water, causing her breasts to lift and strain against the fabric, making his mouth go dry.

"—in the washing machine?"

He turned quickly, so that she wouldn't catch him staring. "I'm sorry, what did you say?"

"I asked if you could keep an eye on Cody while I go toss these towels in the washing machine," she said.

"I'll do it," he said, grabbing the towels from her and beating a hasty retreat, grateful for the opportunity to escape the temptation of her nearness.

Max found Beth waiting for the kettle to boil when he walked into the kitchen later that night.

"You couldn't sleep, either?" he guessed.

She shook her head. "I hope I didn't disturb you by moving around in here."

"I didn't hear anything but the leftover pumpkin pie calling my name," Max assured her.

"Are you sure it was pumpkin pie talking?" she asked. "Maybe it was apple."

"It was definitely pumpkin," he told her. "And bourbon whipped cream."

"I finished the pumpkin earlier," she confessed guiltily. "But I didn't know it was the last slice until I saw the empty pie plate after I'd eaten it."

"Was it good?"

"*Really* good," she admitted.

"Eva Stockton makes the best pies in Rust Creek Falls—maybe all of Montana," Max said, opening the door of the pantry. "Which is why I always order an extra one from

Daisy's Donuts in town." He winked at her then as he pulled a baker's box out of the back of the cupboard. "Or two."

She exhaled a sigh, apparently relieved to know that she hadn't deprived him of his coveted late-night snack.

"Do you want a cup of tea with your pie?" she asked, as the boiling kettle automatically shut off.

He cut a generous wedge and transferred it to a plate. "Thanks, but I prefer milk near bedtime."

She opened the fridge to retrieve the milk—and the container of bourbon whipped cream he craved.

"You should put a dollop of this in your tea," Max suggested, as he scooped up a mound of the alcohol-infused topping. "It might help you sleep."

"Maybe too well," she said. "I want to be able to hear Cody when he wakes up."

"Wilder will hear him," he said. "I had the crib set up in the room adjacent to his to ensure it."

"Clever," Beth acknowledged, as she carried her cup of tea to the table.

Max took a seat across from her with his pie and his glass of milk. "Wilder told me that he made an appointment at the clinic for a paternity test."

She nodded as she dunked her tea bag in the hot water. "Eleven o'clock tomorrow morning."

"Waste of time if you ask me," he said.

"I'd never heard your son's name before I saw it written on a sticky note in my sister's apartment." Beth admitted. "So when I did, I googled it."

"And?" Max prompted.

"And I'd think, considering your family's vast wealth, you'd want DNA proof before welcoming a random child into your home."

"Cody isn't a random child," Max said. "He's a Crawford."

"Well, if it's all the same to you, I'd like proof of that before I leave my nephew here."

"Ahh," Max said, and nodded. "This isn't really about Cody, it's about you."

She sipped her tea, perhaps considering his remark, before she responded. "I made a promise to my sister to always be there for him."

"And yet, she brought him here," he pointed out. "Abandoning him and abdicating her own responsibilities."

"She didn't abandon him," Beth denied. "She left Cody with the man she believes is his father."

Though Max could appreciate her wanting to defend her sister, facts were facts.

"She left him on the doorstep," he pointed out. "And I'm sorry if it seems as if I'm judging her too harshly, but I'd argue that a woman who can walk away from her children doesn't deserve to have them."

"Them?" Beth echoed.

"Him." Max cleared his throat. "She doesn't deserve *him*."

She nodded slowly, as if she understood that they were no longer talking about her sister—or not just her sister.

He scowled, none too pleased to realize that his son had spoken to this woman—a virtual stranger—about their painful family history. But of course he had. There was no other reason for her to have picked up on the slip of his tongue except if she knew about Sheila's defection.

And though Beth had admitted to googling Wilder's name, Max wasn't worried that a cursory online search might turn up details of his marriage or divorce. Especially when he'd paid good money to ensure they stayed buried.

"Leighton made a mistake," Beth said now, as she put her empty mug in the dishwasher. "But she'll come back for Cody. You'll see."

Max hoped she was right.

But he sat at the kitchen table with only his disquieting thoughts for company for a long time after Beth had gone upstairs to bed.

He should hit the sack, too. Morning came early and there was a lot of work to be done—especially as he'd directed Wilder to take a break from his usual chores to spend time with Cody. Of course, now that Beth was staying at the Ambling A, Max suspected that she'd assumed primary responsibility for her nephew. But it was good for Wilder to watch and learn, even if he was still in denial about his relationship to the child.

A certain amount of denial was to be expected under the circumstances, but Max anticipated that it would be followed soon by a whole gamut of other emotions. He hoped one of those emotions was anger. Because Wilder should be mad. He should feel ripped off of all the experiences he'd missed because Cody's mother hadn't bothered to tell him that she was going to have his child. He should be furious he'd missed the first four months of the little boy's life. That Leighton had deprived him of the opportunity to be there for his son from the beginning.

Just as Max had deprived Sheila of the opportunity to be there for her children.

He remembered the night of their final confrontation as clearly as if it had just happened.

"I could never love anyone more than I love my children," she insisted, when he accused her of choosing her lover over her family.

"And yet you left here and went to him," he pointed out, his tone dripping with anger and bitterness—but not hurt. He wouldn't let her see the hurt. He would never admit how her betrayal had gutted him.

"You told me to leave. I had nowhere else to go."

He had told her to leave—to get out. But only after she'd confessed that she'd fallen in love with another man.

"You chose him," he said again, confident that he was

on the moral high ground. Maybe he hadn't been the perfect husband, but he hadn't cheated.

"No," she protested. "I didn't choose him. Not over my children. I couldn't. Please, Max, try to understand—"

But Max had been too hurt and angry to understand.

Maybe there had been a tiny part of him that wondered if he was making a mistake, but he didn't allow himself to show any hesitation or doubt. It wasn't in his nature to back down. And it sure as hell wasn't in his nature to give a second chance to the woman who'd betrayed not just him but their family.

But in the end, he was the one who'd been deprived of a second chance to make things right. Because Sheila had signed the divorce papers he sent to her, then died of a broken heart.

A myocardial infarction, actually.

The autopsy would later reveal a previously undiagnosed condition that explained how a thirty-two-year-old woman in otherwise good health could suffer such a tragic event.

But Max knew the truth—he'd killed her.

Chapter Seven

Beth was up early the next morning and feeding Cody his cereal when Wilder came into the kitchen for his first cup of coffee.

"And I thought ranchers were early risers," he remarked, rubbing a hand over his raspy cheek.

The handsome cowboy was dressed in a similar fashion to what he'd been wearing when she first showed up at the ranch—flannel pajama bottoms and a soft cotton T-shirt over hard muscles. His jaw was similarly stubbled, his hair equally tousled. And just like then, her blood hummed in response to his raw masculinity.

"Ranchers have nothing on babies," she told him, pointedly ignoring her body's totally inappropriate reaction.

"Yeah, I learned that yesterday. And the day before," he acknowledged, stifling a yawn. "But I didn't hear him this morning."

"I managed to get to him before he made too much noise," she said.

"I'm pretty sure my father put him in the room next to mine so that I'd have to deal with middle-of-the-night feedings and diaper changes," Wilder remarked.

"And you did all of that the night before," she pointed out. "So it only seemed fair that last night was my turn."

"Do you always try to be fair, Lisbeth?"

"Maybe," she said, wondering how he managed to make fairness sound like a character flaw.

Or maybe she was being overly sensitive—which was definitely one of her character flaws.

"Do you want me to make you some eggs?" she asked, when Wilder opened the refrigerator door and stood for a long moment staring at its contents.

He took out the carton and slammed the fridge door shut again before turning back to face her. "If I want eggs, I can make my own eggs," he snapped at her.

"O-kay," she said, and dipped the plastic spoon into Cody's cereal again.

Because if she was guilty of being overly sensitive, he was just as guilty of being an arrogant jerk.

And apparently he wasn't done being an arrogant jerk, because after pulling a frying pan out of the cupboard he said, "I don't know what you think is happening here, but I have no interest in playing house with you."

"Playing house?" she echoed, torn between bafflement and outrage. "Is that what you think I'm doing—*playing?* Do you honestly think any of this has been *fun* for me?"

Though she kept her voice low so as not to upset her nephew, she made no effort to disguise the fury beneath her words. And when she stood to carry Cody's now empty bowl and spoon to the sink, she felt a grim sense of satisfaction that Wilder actually took a step back, out of her path.

"Let's revisit the most fun parts," she suggested. "Maybe showing up at my sister's apartment and discovering she'd left town without telling me?" She unbuckled the harness that held Cody in his seat, then lifted the baby into her arms. "Or answering her phone and finding out that my infant nephew was in the care of a stranger almost seventeen hundred miles away? And then driving for twenty-eight hours through the darkness of night and all kinds of weather to make sure he was okay—but essentially being held hostage by a man who doesn't even want to believe he's his father?

"You know what? You're right—it's been *so much fun* I almost wish I was back in grade school so I could write an essay on how I spent my Christmas holidays."

And with that parting shot, she turned on her heel and walked out.

He could be a complete ass at times.

Today was apparently one of those times.

Wilder had no defense for his behavior. Sure, he could make excuses—and having a baby dumped on his doorstep would probably be at the top of the list—but his actions and accusations were indefensible.

And if he was truthful, he'd admit that his questions about Cody and his relationship to the kid weren't all that had kept him awake last night or caused his pissy mood today.

He'd been thinking about Leighton, too, as he'd tossed and turned. Wondering why she'd never told him that she was pregnant. Even if she'd had valid reasons then, why had she never reached out after the baby was born? And, if not then, how about when she decided to undertake the drive from Dallas to Rust Creek Falls with the baby in the back seat of her car? Because a phone call at any of those times would have been preferable to no phone call at all.

And though he'd been thinking about Leighton and all the reasons he had to be furious with her as he'd finally drifted off the sleep, he'd dreamed about her sister.

And how screwed up was that?

Sure, Beth was an attractive woman, but she wasn't at all his type.

Not to mention that she was the kid's aunt, and since there was a possibility that he might be the kid's father, imagining her naked just seemed wrong. Because yes, he hadn't just dreamed about her, he'd had a sex dream about her—and woken up with a raging hard-on.

And then, as if that wasn't awkward enough, he'd walked into the kitchen and she was there. All soft eyes and warm smiles and "Do you want me to make you some eggs?"

So of course he'd responded by acting like a complete ass.

Her anger had been completely justified.

And ass that he was, he couldn't help but notice how pretty her eyes were when they flashed with fire, how kissable her lips seemed even while they were berating him.

But now that the caffeine had started to work its way through his system, he at least had the wherewithal to recognize the inappropriateness of his behavior and acknowledge that he owed her an apology.

He looked at the eggs on the counter and wondered if scrambled or fried would taste better with a side of crow.

Then he rummaged through the fridge for bacon. Because everything was better with bacon.

By the time Beth had Cody changed and dressed, ready for his trip to the clinic, she was ready to acknowledge that she may have overreacted.

Not that she wasn't in the right to be mad at Wilder—because she was—but perhaps she could have expressed her feelings a little less forcefully. No doubt it was the uncertainty of the situation that had them both on edge. But they had an appointment at the clinic today, and though she knew they wouldn't get any immediate answers, it was at least a step in the right direction.

"Just to be clear," she said, when she ventured back into the kitchen as Wilder was finishing his breakfast, "I don't want to be here any more than you want me here."

"I know." He cleared his empty plate then pulled a chair away from the table. "Sit down. Please."

She strapped Cody into his car seat first, and then she sat. Her puzzled gaze shifted from the folded napkin and cutlery to the steaming mug of fresh coffee with a splash of cream—and finally the plate of food he set in front of her.

"What's this?" she asked warily, as if the crisp bacon and scrambled eggs might, in fact, be something else.

"An apology," he said, proving her suspicion was correct.

She lifted the fork and poked at the eggs, as if she didn't quite trust that his culinary offering was a sincere effort to make amends.

"We don't keep any arsenic in the kitchen," he assured her.

"Why are you apologizing?" she asked, after she'd nipped the end off a slice of bacon.

"Because I was mad at your sister and I took it out on you."

His honesty was as surprising as his apparent contrition, and equally appreciated. Beth sampled the eggs, then nodded. "Apology accepted."

"Really?" Now it was his turn to sound skeptical. "Just like that?"

"I'm not too happy with Leighton right now myself," she acknowledged, still unable to understand why, if her sister was finding parenting such a challenge, she hadn't reached out to Beth.

But even as the question formed in her mind, she ruefully acknowledged the answer. Because Leighton had always viewed Beth as the favorite child, a rule follower who did everything right, even following in their mother's footsteps and becoming a kindergarten teacher. Leighton, on the other hand, liked to break the rules and had even dropped out of high school when she was sixteen to sing in a band.

They'd traveled across the country, en route to Seattle, playing in bars that paid them in free drinks, not caring that most of the band members were underage. Leighton had made it as far as Twin Falls, Idaho, before deciding that she'd had enough of eating fast food and sleeping in a rusty van.

Of course, she didn't come home with her tail between her legs. Regret and remorse had never been her style. Instead, she'd regaled Beth with outrageous stories about the things she'd seen and done, taking pleasure in shocking her straitlaced sister.

Their parents had only heard about half of the stories, but that had been enough to shock them, too. Eager to create some distance between their younger daughter and her so-called friends, Alfred and Lucy Ames had encouraged Leighton to spend a few months traveling in Europe.

Such a trip was a luxury beyond the means of their solidly middle-class lifestyle, but they made it work by cashing in Leighton's college fund. Since she'd given no indication that she was interested in even graduating from high school at the time, it seemed a better use of the money.

As Beth had mentioned to Wilder, Leighton eventually got her GED but she was still happy to work as a bartender, boasting that she could make more money in tips in one night than Beth made in a week working with "snotty-nosed little kids."

And wasn't it ironic that Beth, who'd always dreamed of marrying and having a family, was still single and alone, while Leighton, who never wanted to be tied down, had been blessed with a beautiful, perfect baby?

"So we're good?" Wilder prompted, drawing her attention back to the present.

"We're good," she said. "But if we don't get a move on, we're going to be late."

She was a little nervous about taking the baby into a clinic potentially full of sick people. Though Cody was as up-to-date with his immunizations as he could be at four and a half months, Beth still worried about unnecessary exposure to germs and viruses.

The Rust Creek Falls Clinic was bright and clean with friendly and efficient staff. While Wilder filled out the necessary paperwork, Beth sat Cody on her knee, gently jiggling her leg to keep him moving so he wouldn't fuss while they waited.

Thankfully, they didn't have to wait long. When the doctor came in to the exam room, he explained how the test worked, asked if they had any questions, then completed the procedure.

Wilder volunteered to go first, so that Cody could see how it was done. He showed no outward hesitation, but Beth sensed his wariness, though she suspected it was related to the potential results rather than the requirements of the test itself.

The doctor opened the sterile package, the potential daddy opened his mouth, and the inside of his cheek was swabbed. The swab with the collected sample was then deposited in a tube and sealed up again.

Cody was less cooperative on his turn. He didn't understand the concept of keeping his mouth open for the doctor to complete his task, and he didn't seem to approve of either the taste or the texture of what was in his mouth. Several times he clamped his jaw down on the wooden stick, prompting the doctor to remark that it was a good thing the baby didn't yet have any teeth. Still, it didn't take long for the doctor to be satisfied that he had an adequate sample, and less than half an hour after entering the clinic, they were exiting again.

"That was almost anticlimactic," Beth remarked, as she walked beside Wilder to his truck.

"Now we just have to wait for some computer to analyze the spit on those sticks and decide whether or not I'm the kid's father."

"Something like that," she agreed.

"Doesn't seem like it should take seven to ten days," he grumbled.

"The doctor said it's usually less than a week, but the lab might be backed up because of the holidays."

"I guess that puts a snag in your plans."

She shrugged. "I can't really complain about spending the holidays with my favorite guy."

"I'm flattered," he said.

She shook her head. "You know I wasn't talking about you."

"Yeah," he admitted with a grin. "But I do like to see you blush."

"Am I blushing?" she asked. "I can't tell, because my whole face is frozen."

He chuckled as he opened the passenger-side door of his truck for her.

Of course, she didn't immediately buckle up, because she had to wait for him to set Cody's baby seat in place and double-check that it was securely locked in the base.

"Are you hungry?" he asked, when he slid behind the wheel.

"It seems as if breakfast wasn't that long ago," she said. "But actually, I am hungry."

"You want to grab a bite at the Gold Rush Diner?"

"Sure," she said.

The restaurant wasn't far from the clinic—but according to Wilder, nothing in Rust Creek Falls was too far from anything else. A cowbell rang overhead as they entered, no doubt intended to alert restaurant employees to the comings and goings of customers. Though she would have thought they were ahead of the lunch crowd, several booths and tables were occupied by diners already eating or even finishing their meals.

Beth decided on a booth because she knew Cody's seat

would fit snugly on the red vinyl bench. She wrangled the carrier into place, then unzipped the fleece cover-over top so the baby—who'd been lulled to sleep on the short drive—wouldn't get overheated while they were in the restaurant.

Menus were tucked against the wall, propped up by a tray of condiments. Wilder handed one across the table to her, then took one for himself.

She quickly scanned the offerings, then set the menu aside.

"That was fast," he noted.

"I've had a craving for a spicy chicken sandwich, so I was happy to see it on the menu."

"Sounds good," he decided, and tucked his menu away, too.

A server appeared almost right away. She introduced herself as Raina and started to relay the lunch specials, then she spotted the baby seat and completely lost track of what she was saying in favor of cooing over the sleeping infant.

"See?" Wilder said to Beth, after Raina had finally managed to pull herself together and take their orders.

"What am I supposed to see?"

"The way she oohed and aahed over the baby."

"It happens all the time," Beth said matter-of-factly. "Because he's too adorable for real words."

"Well, my dad would say that's just more proof he's a Crawford," he said immodestly.

"What do you think?"

He shrugged. "I guess we'll know for sure in seven to ten days, won't we?"

"I guess we will," she agreed, as Raina delivered their drinks to the table.

As she sipped her diet cola, she noted interesting details about the decor. But while she looked around the restaurant, she got the uneasy feeling that others were looking at her. Not that anyone was blatantly or obviously staring, but a couple of times, she caught a gaze being quickly averted before connecting with her own.

"Why do I get the feeling people are staring at me?" she asked, whispering across the table to Wilder.

He turned his head so that he had a view of the seating area. "Because they probably are."

"Thanks for the reassurance," she said dryly.

"Or they could be staring at me," he suggested as an alternative, shifting his attention back to her. "Rust Creek Falls is a small town, and newcomers and strangers are equally rare sightings. And there's been a fair amount of talk and speculation about the Texas Crawfords—as we've been dubbed by some members of the community—who plunked down a boatload of cash for the Ambling A."

"How much is a boatload?" she wondered aloud.

"Are you looking for the specific number?" Wilder asked.

Beth immediately shook her head. "No, I'm only pointing out that 'boatload' is an incredibly imprecise measure," she told him. "I mean, a boat filled with singles wouldn't necessarily be a lot of money—unless it was a really big boat. On the other hand, a smaller boat filled with C-notes could be a significant amount."

He chuckled at that. "Fair point."

"But if the other diners are staring at you—Wilder Crawford from Texas with boatloads of money—they're probably also speculating about your relationship to the baby that your father insists looks so much like a Crawford no one would guess he was anything else."

"No doubt the gossip is spreading like wildfire," he agreed.

"That doesn't bother you?"

He shrugged. "I try not to be bothered by things that are out of my control."

"That's a very Zen attitude," she noted.

"Plus, there is a silver lining," he said.

"What's that?"

"Rumors that I knocked up an old flame in Dallas and moved away to shirk the responsibility of fatherhood might discourage the local women who have set their sights on snagging the last Crawford bachelor from Texas."

"Are such rumors going around?" she asked, immediately concerned for his reputation.

"No," he admitted. "But I haven't given up hope yet."

She shook her head despairingly. "Is it really such a trial to be sought after by a few young ladies in the community?"

"It is when 'sought after' becomes 'hunted'—which is what happened when my father put a bounty on my head."

"A bounty?" she echoed dubiously.

He nodded. "Max offered a ridiculous sum of money to a local matchmaker to find marriageable women for each of his sons."

She couldn't imagine that any of the Crawford brothers had ever needed help snagging a woman's attention. Though she hadn't yet met all of Wilder's siblings, there were enough photos around the house to prove they were a good-looking group. In her opinion, Wilder was the most handsome of the bunch, but none of them was hard on the eyes. And according to Avery, each one was as charming as he was good looking.

But her curiosity was piqued by his revelation, prompting her to ask, "An honest-to-goodness matchmaker?"

"Well, technically she's a wedding planner, but that didn't stop her from embracing the challenge. And though she hasn't had much success, every one of my brothers has gotten engaged or married since we moved to Rust Creek Falls."

"How long ago did you move here?" she asked him.

"Six months."

"You're kidding."

This time he shook his head. "Barely more than a month after a chance meeting at the matchmaker's office, Logan married Sarah at the Ace in the Hole and became an instant daddy to baby Sophia. Then Xander fell in love with Lily, though she was originally identified as a prospective match for Knox."

"Lily and Knox didn't hit it off?" she guessed.

"They never had a chance to hit it off. Knox decided to be a no-show for the blind date Vivienne had arranged, so Xander went in his place and the rest, as they say, is history. Very recent history, in this case."

"What happened next?" Beth wanted to know.

"Well, our dad was starting to feel pretty smug about two of his sons finding their matches in short order, so Knox married Gen to teach him a lesson about interfering in his life."

"That seems like an extreme response," she noted.

"And one with very unexpected consequences."

She held her breath, waiting for the reveal.

"They fell in love," he concluded.

"Unexpected but happy consequences," she decided.

"Maybe. Depending on your point of view."

"You don't think they're happy?"

"No, they are happy," he confirmed. "I just don't think falling in love is always a happy consequence."

"Have you ever been in love?"

"I'm too steady on my feet to fall," he told her, adding a cocky wink for good measure.

She rolled her eyes at that as she sipped her diet cola. "Okay, so that's three of your brothers."

He nodded before continuing his narrative. "Finn was the next—or maybe he was the first, because he'd actually hooked up with Avery in Dallas before we moved to Montana, but they only got married a couple months ago.

Their second wedding—after they'd already eloped—was a big, splashy affair in Rustler's Notch, Colorado. We convinced Hunter to bring a nanny along to help out with his daughter so he could have some grown-up fun, and now he's engaged to the nanny."

"But going back to Logan and Sarah, it all started with the visit to the matchmaker," Beth pointed out. "So maybe she's done a better job than you're giving her credit for."

And though it wasn't something she'd ever considered before, it occurred to her now that enlisting a professional to help her find a life partner might not be such a bad idea. Because as much as she wanted to believe that her perfect match was out there waiting for her, she was twenty-eight years old and starting to doubt her ability to find him on her own.

"Or she's secretly serving Homer Gilmore's spiked wedding punch to her clients," Wilder muttered.

"What?"

He waved a hand dismissively. "Never mind. That's another long story."

"So has this matchmaker turned her attention to finding a match for you now?"

"If she has, she's destined for failure there," he said. "Because I have no interest in being matched by her—and even less in being manipulated by my father."

"Leighton always balked at being told what to do, too," Beth noted. "Which is why I was so surprised to learn that she'd brought Cody to Montana, because from day one, I'd been urging her to contact his father."

"Why do you think she decided to listen to you now?"

"I don't know," Beth admitted. "But I don't doubt that she was doing what she thought was best for Cody."

"Do you really think she'll come back?" he asked, as Raina approached with their meals.

"I know she will," Beth said, attempting to project more

confidence in her voice than she actually felt. Because she wanted to believe it was true, though after five of days with no communication from her sister, she was beginning to have some doubts of her own.

Cody woke up when the server set their plates on the table, almost as if he expected there to be food for him, too. Instead, Beth gave him a pacifier to keep him busy—and quiet.

Still, his eyes followed her hand as she picked up a fry and moved it toward her mouth. Watching him, she chuckled softly. "Yeah, I bet you'd like to try these, wouldn't you? But you need a couple of teeth before you'll be ready to tackle something like this—although the way you've been gnawing on that pacifier, I wouldn't be surprised if the first ones aren't too far in the distance."

"When do babies usually get teeth?" Wilder asked.

"Usually around the six-month mark, but first teeth can show up as early as three months or as late as the first birthday."

"How do you know so much about these things?" he wondered.

"I read a lot."

"All those books you bought for Leighton?" he guessed.

She frowned. "Why do you assume I bought them?"

"Am I wrong?"

"No," she admitted. "I just wondered why you leaped to that conclusion."

"I won't pretend that I knew your sister very well, but based on what I did know about her, she wasn't the type to read about something if she could do it."

"I think that's why she asked me to be her birthing partner," Beth said. "Because she knew I'd study the course materials and take notes in childbirth classes, so it wouldn't matter if she didn't pay attention because I'd be there to talk her through it."

"So you were there—when she had the baby?"

"Yeah." She looked at Cody and smiled at the memory of his face all scrunched up and red as he screamed at the indignity of being born. "I was there."

He picked up his burger, bit into it.

She didn't offer any more detailed information, because she wasn't sure how much he'd want to know.

But when he'd finished chewing and swallowed, he asked, "What was it like?"

"The birth?"

He nodded.

"Long and sweaty and messy." She smiled again. "And the most amazing thing I've ever seen."

"How long?" he wondered.

"Sixteen hours," she said. "Leighton was a trouper through it all. There were a few scary moments when labor stalled and they considered a C-section, but she pushed through."

She'd thought her sister was afraid of being cut open—a not unreasonable fear—and only found out after the fact that what her sister had feared most was the possibility of a scar that might prevent her from wearing a bikini at the beach.

And though a lot of people might think it a shallow rationale, Beth understood the root of her sister's insecurities. Because while Leighton had struggled in school, she'd quickly learned that being "such a beautiful child" had a certain intrinsic value—and she'd capitalized on it. She wasn't just pretty, she was popular. While Lisbeth spent her evenings at home with her head stuck in a book, Leighton was usually out with friends.

Because she had been known as "Lisbeth" back then. After all, it was what her parents had always called her and the name they'd put on her birth certificate. But the summer before Lisbeth started high school, Leighton had suddenly started calling her "Beth."

The reason, she explained without apology, was that she didn't want it to be so obvious to her friends and the other popular kids at school that they were sisters. Even though Lisbeth would be in her junior year by the time her sister was a freshman, Leighton had no doubt that she'd be immediately accepted by the in-crowd and didn't want anyone to connect her with "Little Miss Perfect."

Beth could have protested, but dropping the first syllable of her name seemed like a small thing to help her sister. Or maybe she felt as if she owed her something, because learning had always come so easily to Beth while Leighton had struggled to attain good grades.

As a result, her sister had learned to exploit her other attributes. Unfortunately, those attributes were superficial, so that even when she was laboring to bring new life into the world, she wasn't able to embrace and celebrate that miracle without worrying about stretch marks and scars that might diminish her sense of self-worth.

"But Leighton battled through," Beth said, continuing her explanation of her sister's labor to Wilder. "And, a few hours later, Cody was born weighing seven pounds ten ounces and measuring nineteen and a half inches. He also had a sprinkling of dark hair and a very healthy set of lungs." She smiled at the memory of those lungs announcing his arrival to everyone in the maternity wing of the hospital, then her smile faded as she looked at Wilder across the table. "I'm sorry you weren't given the option to be there."

"So am I," he said.

"Would you have wanted to be there?" she asked, surprised by the sincere regret she heard in his tone.

"I would have stepped up," he assured her.

"That's not what I asked."

He took a long sip of his cola, then he nodded. "Yeah," he said. "I would have wanted to be there."

Before she could say anything else, Raina appeared to clear away their empty plates.

"Can I get you anything for dessert?" the server asked.

Wilder looked at Beth, who shook her head.

"No, thanks," he said. "Just the check."

He reached into his back pocket for his wallet as the server returned with the requested check.

But Beth was quicker, having already slid her credit card out of her wallet, and she immediately offered it as payment.

"What are you doing?" Wilder protested.

"Buying you lunch," she told him. "It's the least I can do, considering that I'm not paying to stay at your place."

"Fine, I'll let you buy lunch," he relented. "But you can't take out your wallet again for the rest of the day."

Chapter Eight

"You said you wanted to go to *the* General Store," Beth remarked as they entered. "You didn't mention that it was *Crawford's* General Store."

"But I did warn you about walking down Sawmill Street and bumping into my relatives," he reminded her, as they approached a pretty blonde at the checkout counter. "And this one is my third cousin twice removed, or something like that."

"But you can call me Natalie," the clerk said, with a warm smile.

"And this is Beth," Wilder said, continuing the introductions.

"It's nice to meet you," Beth said automatically.

But the other woman had already turned her attention to the car seat in Wilder's hand. "And I'm guessing this is Cody," she said, crouching for a closer look at the baby. "Maggie told me there was a new baby at the Ambling A."

Beth looked questioningly at Wilder.

"Maggie's married to Natalie's brother Jesse," he told her. "Maggie and Jesse loaned us the crib and rocking chair."

Beth nodded, recognizing the names now that she had a context.

"So what brings you in today?" Natalie asked. "Just making the rounds through town to meet the family?"

"Beth's having enough trouble adjusting to the Montana weather. I don't think she needs the shock of being subjected to our family."

"The Crawfords aren't so bad," Natalie said, then winked at Beth. "Although I've heard some rumors about the Dallas branch of the family tree."

Her warm smile and easy manner immediately put Beth at ease.

Wilder ignored Natalie's teasing remark. "We're here because Beth needs some underwear," he said.

And that quickly, Beth's feeling of ease vanished.

"What?" She squawked the question as her cheeks grew hot. She'd only had one extra pair of panties in her duffel bag, because she'd only planned on spending one night at her sister's, but how could Wilder know that?

"Long underwear," he clarified.

But Beth still couldn't look at him. Couldn't believe that this cowboy she'd known all of two days had brought her here to shop for underwear—even if only the thermal kind.

"Beth's from Dallas," he continued his explanation. "So she's ill-prepared for our winter."

"You're the little guy's mom?" the other woman guessed.

"His aunt," Beth clarified.

"Oooh, plot twist," Natalie said gleefully.

Wilder rolled his eyes.

"How long are you going to be in Rust Creek Falls?" Natalie asked Beth.

"Seven to ten days, apparently."

"Then you're going to need a real coat," the clerk told her. "And some decent footwear, too."

Beth's frigid toes automatically curled inside her unlined boots.

"Avery said she's got a down-filled jacket that Beth can borrow," Wilder said. "Since she can't get it zipped up over her belly right now, anyway."

"She's probably got a dozen pairs of boots, too," Natalie guessed.

"But her feet are bigger than Beth's."

"And how do you know that?" Beth demanded.

"Because I asked."

"You didn't ask me."

"No, I looked at the label inside your boots," he acknowledged. "You wear a seven, Avery's a nine. But Sarah said she's got a pair of size eights you can borrow."

"A pair of thick socks would make those work," Natalie noted.

"She's going to want some of those, too," Wilder said.

"*She* would very much appreciate being able to decide what she does and doesn't need," Beth said pointedly.

"I'm only trying to help."

"A coffee run would be helpful," Natalie said.

"I don't want coffee," he said.

"Well, I do," the clerk said. "More importantly, I don't think Beth wants you hovering while she picks out underwear."

"Thank you," Beth said when Wilder had finally gone.

The other woman smiled. "Sometimes men are so clueless, blunt is the only option."

"It was kind of Wilder to consider what I might need," Beth allowed. "But it is a little awkward to discuss undergarments with a man I barely know."

"Agreed," Natalie said. "Now the key to surviving a Montana winter is layers. Long underwear refers to thermal undergarments that you wear over your usual underwear and under your clothes."

"I know what long underwear is," Beth said. "I just—"

"Got flustered by a handsome cowboy talking about your underwear?" Natalie teased.

Beth's cheeks burned hotter. "Apparently."

The other woman grinned. "So you *do* think he's handsome?"

"I also need regular underwear," she confided, ignoring Natalie's question. She did not want to discuss Wilder's handsomeness or acknowledge—even to herself—that her knees turned to jelly every time he stood a little too close. "I didn't plan on being gone more than a single night, so I've only got one spare."

"We don't have a great selection," Natalie confided. "Anyone who wants sexy stuff either goes shopping in Kalispell or orders online from Victoria's Secret, but we do have some cotton bikinis with lace trim."

"I'm not looking for sexy," Beth hastened to assure her. "No one's going to see my underwear but me."

"Well, that's unfortunate," Natalie teased.

And Beth realized that she was right.

In fact, it wasn't just unfortunate but a little sad that she had no concerns about a man seeing her intimate apparel, because it meant that she had no prospects on the horizon for a relationship. But until she sorted out the situation with Cody, that was the way it was going to have to be.

Beth was standing at the checkout counter when Wilder returned to the store with Natalie's requested macchiato.

"What do you think you're doing?" he demanded, as she started to hand her credit card across the counter.

"Paying for my clothes," she said.

He shook his head. "You agreed to put your wallet away for the rest of the day."

"That was before I knew we were coming here."

"A deal's a deal," he insisted, handing the to-go cup to Natalie along with his platinum credit card.

"I wouldn't have agreed to get half this stuff if I'd known you were going to insist on paying for it," Beth felt compelled to protest.

"He can afford it," Natalie said, with a dismissive wave of her hand, obviously aware he had boatloads of money. "All of this and a lot more. In fact, you should get that other pair of jeans you tried on."

Beth shook her head. "I don't need more than one pair."

But Wilder vetoed her decision. "Add the other pair of jeans," he said to Natalie.

"I don't need them," Beth said again, even as they were added to the pile.

"At least this proves you're different from the other women Wilder has been seen with around town," Natalie said, processing the transaction.

"How so?" she asked, a little warily.

"Because he's buying clothes for you instead of taking them off you."

"Thanks for your help, Nat," Wilder said dryly, snatching his receipt out of her hand.

She winked. "Anytime."

When they got back to the Ambling A, Wilder mixed up a bottle of formula while Beth took her new clothes up to the guest room. She did feel a little strange, letting a man she barely knew—and a former lover of her sister—buy her clothes, but, as he'd argued on the drive, what he'd paid for today didn't begin to repay her for everything she'd done for Cody.

Not that she wanted repayment. Everything she'd done for her nephew had been done out of love. But equating the shopping trip today to packages of diapers and cans of formula, she felt a little less guilty about the money he'd spent.

When her new clothes were stored away, she crossed the hall to the makeshift nursery to ask Wilder a question. The query slipped from her mind, forgotten, as her gaze settled on the handsome cowboy giving a bottle to the baby cuddled against his chest.

She saw it then—not just the physical resemblance between the man and the child that Max kept insisting was obvious, but how right they looked together.

Father and son.

Wilder might be quick to point out that the familial relationship was yet unproven, but looking at them now, seeing how the baby was carefully cradled in the crook of his arm, seeing the earnestness of his expression, she no longer doubted that the man cared about her nephew. And in that moment, though she was still frustrated with her sister for the way she'd handled things, she had to consider that maybe Leighton had done the right thing in bringing Cody here.

She watched Wilder ease the bottle from the baby's mouth before shifting Cody to his shoulder, his big hand gently rubbing the tiny back, and her heart swelled inside her chest.

But even if Leighton had done the right thing, where was she now? And why hadn't she been in touch?

Because it was one thing for Leighton to invoke radio silence with respect to her sister, but she should want to reach out to the man with whom she'd left her baby.

Wasn't she the least bit worried about Cody?

And if she wasn't, she should be.

Because as Beth had discovered when she showed up at the Ambling A, the handsome cowboy could barely manage a diaper change.

Of course, he'd come a long way since then, but Leighton had no way of knowing that.

Leighton had no way of knowing anything because she hadn't been in communication with anyone.

Which Beth knew because she'd kept a close eye on her sister's social media accounts, messaged her friends and reached out to her boss—to no avail. She'd even contacted the authorities in Dallas to inquire about filing a missing person's report. But after summarizing the situation, she'd been told that since her sister had have left of her own free will, Beth should hire a private investigator if she really wanted to track her down—an idea that she was keeping in her back pocket for now.

Desperate for a distraction, she retreated to the kitchen to figure out something for the evening meal.

She'd been a little surprised to discover that the obviously wealthy family didn't have a full-time housekeeper-slash-cook. When she'd asked Wilder about it, he told her that the woman who'd filled those roles in Dallas had declined to make the move to Rust Creek Falls with them. Although she'd worked for Max for almost thirty years and had been like a surrogate mother to his six sons, she had children and grandchildren of her own in Texas and no desire to move so far away from them.

Max had promised to advertise for a cook when they moved into the Ambling A, but during the summer months, it had been easy enough to throw some meat on the grill. So while there was a housekeeper who came in twice a week to tidy up, the men of the Ambling A had mostly fended for themselves when it came to meals—or gone into town to eat.

Of course, now that five of his sons were married or headed in that direction, the responsibility for meals in the main house fell to the patriarch and his youngest son. As a result, they'd eaten a lot of steaks, burgers and pasta over the past several months—unless they were fortunate enough to have Lily prepare a meal for them.

With that thought in mind, Beth rummaged through the freezer looking for some inspiration.

She was chopping carrots and celery when Wilder came down to the kitchen with Cody's empty bottle in one hand

and the baby monitor he'd borrowed from another of his relatives in the other.

"We didn't have lunch all that long ago," he noted. "Are you hungry already?"

"Ha ha," she said. "I'm making stew for dinner."

"You know you don't have to cook for us, don't you?"

"I know," she agreed. "But I'm sleeping in your house and eating your food, so it seems the least I can do is put a meal on the table."

"You made meatloaf last night," he reminded her.

"Are you suggesting that because you had dinner last night you won't want to eat tonight?"

"Of course not," he said.

"Is it that you don't like stew?"

"Stew's basically meat and potatoes in gravy, right? What's not to like?"

"Good," she said, and gestured to the bag on the counter. "You can peel the potatoes."

Max came in a few hours later, stomping to knock the snow off his boots. "Forecast says we could get another four to six inches of the white stuff tonight," he remarked.

"Oh, goody," Beth said dryly.

The old man chuckled as he removed his boots. "Missing Dallas yet?"

"I was missing Dallas by the time I hit Colorado Springs."

"What's cooking?" Max asked, hanging his coat and hat on a hook by the door.

"Beef stew."

"It sure does smell good," he said.

"Hopefully it tastes as good."

"It does," Wilder said. At her questioning look, he shrugged. "I had to sample it for quality control purposes."

"Well, don't sample till it's done," Max said. "I'm hoping there will be some left over for my lunch tomorrow."

Please help make our
"Fast Five" Reader Survey
a success!

Dear Reader,

Since you are a lover of our books, your opinions are important to us... and so is your time.

That's why we made sure your **"FAST FIVE" READER SURVEY** can be completed in just a few minutes. Your answers to the five questions will help us remain at the forefront of women's fiction.

And, as a thank-you for participating, we'd like to send you **4 FREE THANK-YOU GIFTS!**

Enjoy your gifts with our appreciation,

Pam Powers

"Why would I venture outside in this ridiculous weather to buy something I could make right here?" she countered.

"It took me some time to adjust to the cold, too," he acknowledged. "But a rancher doesn't have the option of sheltering inside when there are animals to be tended to."

"Then it's a good thing I'm not a rancher."

"We'll get you out enjoying the snow yet," he said.

"Don't count on it," she said.

"Have you ever taken a ride in a horse-drawn sleigh?"

"No," she said. "And if your next question is, 'Have you ever wanted to ride in a horse-drawn sleigh?'—the answer would be 'no' again."

"I bet Cody would get a kick out of it," he said.

Her gaze narrowed. "Oh, now you're fighting dirty."

"I'm not fighting at all," he denied. "But I am surprised that you'd let your nephew miss out on an enjoyable activity just so that you can stay warm."

She huffed out a breath. "Fine," she relented. "We'll go tomorrow."

He grinned. "Don't forget your thermal underwear."

Chapter Nine

Beth stood at the window, looking out at the pristine landscape. The promised four to six inches had arrived overnight, so that everything was covered in a fresh blanket of white.

"It does look pretty," Beth said to Cody.

She was holding him with his back to her front, so he could see what she was seeing. He reached out to put his hand on the glass, then quickly pulled it back again.

"That's the problem," she said. "As pretty as it looks, it has to be cold for that white stuff not to melt."

"It's not that cold out today," Wilder said, joining their conversation as he entered the room.

"I don't see the snow melting," she remarked.

He smiled. "No, the snow's not melting," he agreed. "So go put on your coat and boots while I get Cody bundled up for his first sleigh ride."

She appreciated the way the words "first sleigh ride" rolled off his tongue. As if he anticipated there would be a second and a third. As if he wanted the little boy to spend more winters here in Rust Creek Falls with him. Maybe all the other seasons, too.

For herself, she expected that this would be her first and her last sleigh ride. And though she suspected she'd be too preoccupied with her frozen fingers and toes to enjoy it, a promise was a promise.

She'd put on a pair of thermal underwear that morning, as instructed, then added a long-sleeved shirt and a thick sweater, blue jeans and two pairs of socks. Cody was similarly dressed in layers, and Wilder had borrowed a down-filled bunting bag with built-in mittens and a faux fur-trimmed hood for the little guy.

In the foyer, she shoved her feet into the boots she'd borrowed from Sarah, wrapped herself in Avery's jacket, pulled a knitted hat over her head, wound a scarf around her neck, and slid her hands into fleece-lined mittens, all accessories courtesy of Lily.

Wilder chuckled. "You really are a tenderfoot, aren't you?"

"And not ashamed to admit it," she told him, her voice muffled through the scarf already pulled up to cover her mouth.

"Let's get out of here before you overheat," he suggested.

She nodded and followed Wilder and Cody out the door.

Though she braced herself for the cold air, she forgot about the weather altogether for a brief moment when she spotted the pair of enormous black horses harnessed to a fancy black sleigh with glossy-painted red runners, a tufted red velvet seat and collapsible roof.

"Did you steal Santa's ride?" she asked Wilder.

"I'm pretty sure that would get my name on the naughty list, so no," he said. "This is actually an antique doctor's sleigh."

"So you stole it from an old doctor?"

He chuckled. "That would be another no. My dad bought it, restored, at an auction."

"It's beautiful," she said, stroking a mittened hand over the curved side.

"And it rides incredibly smooth," he promised. "Of course, you have to actually get in the sleigh before we can go anywhere."

He offered his hand, and she stepped up into the sleigh.

"There aren't any seat belts," she realized, as she lowered herself onto the seat.

"Seat belts hadn't been invented when this sleigh was made," he pointed out, passing her the bundled baby. "But it's perfectly safe, I promise."

She nibbled on her lower lip as she hugged Cody close to her body, uneasy with the idea of taking her nephew for any kind of ride without him being secured in an NHTSA-approved child restraint system.

"You're not convinced?" he guessed.

"I'm a worrywart," she reminded him.

"There's nothing wrong with being cautious," he said. "But trust me, I wouldn't have suggested this ride if I wasn't one hundred percent certain that Cody would be safe. Although I can try to rig up some kind of anchor system for his car seat, if that would make you feel better."

It would make her feel better. But she couldn't imagine how they'd both fit in the sleigh with the baby's bulky car seat between them. And maybe she needed to learn to be a little less rigid all the time.

"You're one hundred percent certain?" she asked, seeking reassurance.

"One hundred percent," he confirmed.

"And you won't go too fast?"

"I'll go as slow as you need me to go," he said, with a teasing wink.

"Okay, then." She decided to ignore his double entendre as she tightened her arms around the baby. "Let's go for a ride."

He settled beside her and picked up the reins, and she felt a little niggle of fear as she shifted forward in her seat when the animals began to move. But their gait was slow and steady, the ride as smooth as Wilder had promised, and she soon relaxed again.

As the sleigh traveled over the snow-covered ground,

he identified the other buildings on the property and described their specific uses, pointed out the cabins belonging to his brothers, and answered her curious and numerous questions about raising the cattle she could see in the distance.

"Now are you willing to admit that this was worth leaving the house for?" he asked, as he paused the horses at the top of a hill for an overview of the sprawling property.

"More than," she agreed, as she turned her head to admire the pristine beauty of the land in every direction. "Is all of this really yours?"

He chuckled. "Not mine, but everything you can see, all the way to that fence—" he pointed to a barrier in the distance "—is the Ambling A."

"You really like it here, don't you?"

"I thought I'd miss being close to the city when we moved," Wilder confided. "And I did, at first. But it's amazing how quickly I adjusted to being out here."

"'Out here' being the middle of nowhere?" she guessed.

He grinned. "It's not so bad."

"There's not even a movie theater in town."

"They show movies in the high school gym on Friday and Saturday nights—so long as one of the sports teams isn't playing."

"Oh, well, I had no idea," she said. "Movies in the high school gym? This town is practically a booming metropolis."

"And for anyone who can't live without a real movie theater experience, Kalispell is only half an hour away."

"Kalispell isn't Dallas," she pointed out. "It isn't a quarter the size of Dallas."

"Life's about choices,' he said. "My dad chose to come here and, as much as he drives me crazy sometimes, I wanted to support that choice."

"You're a good son, Wilder Crawford."

"That's kind of you to say. Of course, being a good son doesn't necessarily equate to being a good father, does it?"

"Not necessarily," she agreed. "But it never hurts to have a positive role model."

"It couldn't have been easy for my dad, having to parent six rowdy sons on his own, but he did it," Wilder acknowledged. "I respect and admire that, but I wish he'd accept that we're grown-ups now and let us live our own lives."

"Is this about the matchmaker again?" she guessed.

"Among other things."

The cryptic response didn't invite further discussion, so she only said, "Well, thank you for bringing me and Cody out here. It really was an unforgettable experience."

"It was my pleasure," he said, then smiled as he glanced at the sleeping baby. "But I don't know that Cody got much out of it."

"If nothing else, he got some fresh air."

"One of my favorite things about being a rancher is working outdoors," Wilder confided. "I could never imagine myself stuck in an office from nine to five."

"But as a rancher, you often work longer hours than that, don't you?"

"And seven days a week," he agreed.

"So if it turns out that you are Cody's father, how would you juggle that schedule with the demands of parenting?" she asked.

"I don't know," he admitted. "But I know my family will help. And Cody's only one baby. There's another rancher in town—Jamie Stockton—who was widowed with infant triplets."

"That must have been overwhelming," she acknowledged.

"You'd think so," he agreed. "But that's the thing about a town like Rust Creek Falls—the community comes together to take care of its own."

"Didn't you just move here six months ago?"

"Yeah," he confirmed. "But I already feel as if I've lived here forever."

"Of course, that might have something to do with the fact that you share a last name with half the town's residents."

He chuckled. "Not quite half, but that's a valid point."

"So you don't have any doubts that you'd be able to handle it?"

"Are you kidding? I've got a ton of doubts. But I've never backed down in the face of a challenge."

Then, because he didn't want to think about all those doubts, he reached over and gently nudged her chin up. "Look."

"Oh." Her eyes sparkled with childlike excitement and her lips curved. "It's snowing again."

He studied her as she watched the big, fluffy flakes that seemed to be floating on the air rather than falling from the sky.

"I've never seen snow like this." She smiled again as a flake landed on her cheek. "It's so pretty."

Looking at her, watching her surprised joy at something as simple as a snowfall, he couldn't deny that she was right. It was pretty. And so was she.

"It's pretty—until you have to shovel it," he said.

"Now who's being a spoilsport?" she teased.

And the curve of those perfectly-shaped lips tempted him to taste them, to discover if they were as soft and sweet as they looked.

But, of course, he didn't. He couldn't.

Because she was Cody's aunt and completely off limits.

"Guilty," he acknowledged, and turned the horses back toward the house.

"Though white Christmases are an anomaly back home,

for some reason snow always makes me think of the holiday."

"'Tis the season."

"And since it doesn't look like Cody and I are going to be heading back to Texas anytime soon, would it be okay if I put his presents under the tree when we get back?"

"Of course," he agreed. "And while you're doing that, I'll make the hot chocolate."

Wilder stacked logs and built a fire in the hearth while Beth arranged Cody's presents under the tree, then he went to the kitchen to make the hot chocolate.

He returned to the family room with two steaming mugs topped with marshmallows just in time to catch her brushing an errant tear from her cheek.

"Everything okay?" he asked.

"Under the circumstances, everything is better than okay," she told him.

"So why are you crying?"

"I'm not," she denied, as she accepted the proffered mug.

"You just wiped away a tear."

"A single tear isn't crying," she said.

"So what is it?" he pressed.

"Proof that the holidays make me a little emotional," she confided. "Christmas is my favorite time of year, but it's a bittersweet time, too, because I can't help but remember all the happy Christmases of my childhood, which makes me think about my parents, and then I find myself missing them and—" she cut herself off then. "Oh, Wilder, I'm sorry."

"Why?"

"Because I know you lost your mom, too."

"I didn't lose her—she left," he reminded her.

"And she didn't stay in touch after the divorce?" she asked curiously.

"She died only a few months after the papers were signed."

She wanted to apologize again for bringing up such a difficult subject, but he would only deny it was difficult. Instead she said, "I'm sorry you don't have any memories of her."

He shrugged. "And since I don't, there's nothing for me to miss."

To Beth, that was just as sad.

"So what were your Christmases like?" she asked, hoping he might share some happy memories.

"Nothing out of the ordinary. Presents under the tree, a big turkey dinner. Christmas cookies," he said, and smiled then. "Our housekeeper made these amazing cookies decorated with icing and colored sugars.

"I thought we'd miss out this year, but she sent a box in the mail. There must have been six dozen cookies, and they were gone within two days."

"Not just between you and your dad?"

"No," he admitted. "The note said we had to share, so we did."

She smiled at the obvious regret in his tone. "What about your tree—have you always had a real one?"

"Is there another kind?"

She tapped a finger against one of the branches, watched the tip bob. "They do smell good," she confided.

"You don't get a real tree?" he guessed.

She shook her head. "My apartment's on the sixth floor, and it just seems like too much hassle to drag one into the building, cram it into an elevator, then haul it down the hall and into my apartment, leaving a path of needles along the way."

"A path of needles would make it easy for Santa to find you," he pointed out.

"Instead, I have a sign that goes in the window that says Santa, Please Stop Here!"

"You don't think Saint Nick knows where he's supposed to stop?"

"I don't like leaving some things to chance."

"And what was on your wish list for Santa this year?" Wilder asked her.

"Oh, um, just…you know…the usual stuff."

"You didn't make a list for Santa, did you?"

"Not exactly."

His gaze narrowed thoughtfully. "But there was something specific you wanted," he guessed.

"I just wanted to spend Christmas with Leighton and Cody—to be part of the happy memories of his first Christmas."

"You do know he's not going to remember his first Christmas when he's older?"

"I know," she admitted. "But I've been taking pictures of every event and milestone, to make a scrapbook of his first year, so that he'll be able to look back and know, even if he can't remember."

"You should have asked me to take a picture of the two of you in the sleigh," he told her.

"I was so mesmerized by the sleigh and the horses, I didn't even think about it," she confided.

"Next time," he promised.

But they both knew there might not be a next time, because Beth's days at the Ambling A were numbered—seven to ten—and the countdown was on.

She carefully sipped her hot chocolate and wondered why she didn't seem as excited to anticipate her return to Dallas as she'd been only three days earlier. Goodness knows, she would be happy enough to get back to a place where she didn't need long underwear to step out the front door. But when she did, she might actually miss interacting with Wilder and Max and the various other Crawfords who'd been in and out of the main house at the Ambling A during her brief time there.

She pushed the uncomfortable thought aside and sipped her drink again, savoring the warm sweetness as it slid down her throat. "This is really good," she told Wilder.

"The key ingredients are real cream and dark chocolate," he confided. "And marshmallows on top, of course."

"Of course," she agreed.

"Speaking of marshmallows, you've got some right here," he said, and indicated the location on his own lip.

"Oh." She instinctively sought out the sticky spot with the tip of her tongue. "Did I get it?"

Instead of answering, he reached over and brushed his thumb over the curve of her bottom lip. The callused pad scraped against her soft skin, causing her breath to back up in her lungs and sending tingles through her veins.

She lifted her gaze to find his fixed on her mouth, his head tilted toward her, and for the space of a single heartbeat, she actually thought he was going to kiss her.

And, oh, how she yearned for his kiss. Just the thought of his lips pressed against hers made her tummy feel tingly and her knees grow weak.

But instead of shifting closer, he abruptly pulled away. "It's gone now," he told her.

And then Cody was awake, allowing her to focus on the baby and ignore the twinge of what might have been disappointment.

After she'd snapped a few pictures of Cody propped up against the pile of presents, Wilder took her cell phone and assumed photographer duties while she helped her nephew open his gifts.

There were sleepers and outfits, a pair of high-top running shoes (and of course Wilder questioned the purpose of running shoes for a kid who couldn't even walk), board books and bath books, wooden puzzles and cuddly toys, learning toys and silly toys.

"Let's try these on you," Beth said, tugging off Cody's socks and replacing them with the foot rattles he'd just opened.

One was red-and-orange and decorated to look like a giraffe; the other was black-and-white like a zebra; both had noisemakers sewn into their ears. She put them on his feet and helped him kick his legs to demonstrate how they could make sound.

Cody rewarded her with a gummy smile.

"What's this one?" Wilder asked, picking up a smallish square box wrapped in Santa paper with a red bow.

She took the box from his hand and glanced at the tag that read: To Mommy Love Cody.

"Oh." She managed a smile. "It's a 'Mommy' Christmas ornament, dated for the year Cody was born."

She set it aside and reached for a bigger and flatter package. After carefully prying the tag off the wrapping, she handed the gift to Wilder.

"What's this?"

"A present."

"I know you didn't buy this for me."

"No, I didn't," she acknowledged. "But it's something I'd like you to have."

Curious, he slid a finger beneath the fold of paper to break the tape. The flat, unmarked box didn't give anything away, so he lifted the lid and peeled back the tissue inside to reveal a beautiful brushed silver-tone frame engraved with the words "Cody's First Christmas." Inside the frame was a photo of the baby, asleep in the crook of Santa's arm.

"What a great picture," he said, sincerely touched by her gesture. "This was another gift for your sister?"

"Yeah, but I can get another one made for her," Beth said.

"Is this because you now believe I'm Cody's father?" he asked.

"Do *you* believe it?" she countered.

He looked at the little guy now sitting between his outstretched legs.

Did he believe it?

Were his residual doubts simply a manifestation of his reluctance to take on the responsibilities of fatherhood? Responsibilities that he wouldn't be able to duck if and when he was confirmed to be the baby's father. Not that he'd had much success ducking anything since the baby had appeared on the doorstep and his father had made his own determination about paternity. But doubts aside, the more time he spent with Cody, the less terrifying he found the idea of being his father.

"Well," she said with a shrug, obviously having given up on waiting for an answer. "If it turns out you're not his dad, you can give the picture back to me."

"For now, I'm going to put it right here," he said, propping the frame up on the side table.

Beth looked at the picture there and smiled. "Good choice."

Then she stood up and began gathering the discarded wrapping.

"Somebody lost a sock," Wilder noted, tickling the baby's bare toes as he reached to pick up the giraffe.

Cody giggled.

Beth gasped and spun around, clutching an armload of crumpled paper against her chest. "What did you do?" she asked Wilder.

"Me?" Had he done something wrong? "I just tickled his toes." Then he did it again, to demonstrate for her.

Cody responded with more giggles.

"Oh." The word was barely a whisper from her lips as

her eyes filled with tears. "That's the first time I've heard him laugh."

"Really?" Wilder asked, surprised.

She nodded.

Wilder brushed his fingertips over the bottom of the baby's foot, to see if he was ticklish there. The baby answered with another giggle.

Beth sighed. "Is there anything as sweet as that sound?"

Though she probably wasn't expecting an answer to her question, he heard himself responding, "It's pretty great."

"It makes me happy to know he's happy," she said.

"Of course, he's four months old, so his biggest concerns are a hungry belly or wet diaper," Wilder pointed out.

"And sore gums," she reminded him.

"Still, he's not lying awake at night worrying about the market price of beef," he said, as he worked the sock onto the baby's foot, stroking his fingertip along his sole and sending the little guy into a fresh wave of giggles.

Beth laughed, too, and their gazes met and held for a long moment of shared understanding and unexpected connection.

Then Cody kicked his feet again, shaking the rattles, and the moment was broken.

Chapter Ten

Wilder lay awake in bed for a long time that night, thinking about the day he'd spent with Cody and Beth. He couldn't help but admire Beth's devotion to her nephew and the way she overcame her own reservations to embrace opportunities and new experiences for the little boy. Everything she did seemed to be motivated by his best interests, even before her own wants and needs, her actions a stark contrast to those of her sister, who'd apparently had no qualms about abandoning her child.

Of course, Wilder knew from experience that maternal instincts weren't really instincts in the true sense of the word. They weren't as universal as the compulsion of birds to build nests. While a lot of parents might instinctively bond with, nurture and protect their children, giving birth to a child didn't automatically create or foster such instincts. If it did, his mother never would have walked away, leaving Max to raise their six sons on his own.

Had his father had stronger instincts to care for his children? Or had he only done what needed to be done because his wife's abandonment had left him with no other option?

More important, would Wilder be able to learn everything he needed to know to raise his son—if it turned out that Cody was his son? And why didn't he share Max's conviction that the baby was a Crawford? Was it because he didn't want to be a father to the little guy? Or was he afraid that he would fail in his efforts to be what Cody needed?

"Fatherhood changes everything," Max had told Wilder, when they were alone at the Ambling A after everyone else had gone on Christmas night.

Apparently that was true whether he wanted anything to change or not. And even without any confirmation that he was a father.

At first, he'd been panicked at the idea the kid was his. Now, after spending only a few days with Cody...well, he wasn't quite ready to start handing out cigars with blue bands that proclaimed "It's a Boy," but he wasn't quite so terrified anymore, either. Of course, cigars might be premature, anyway, as he was still waiting on the results of the DNA test.

Maybe he'd feel more of a connection to the kid if he'd known that he existed before he was four months old. If he'd had the opportunity to help Leighton prepare for his arrival. If he'd been there when their baby was born.

He was angry that she'd taken that opportunity away from him. That *she'd* chosen not to tell him about the pregnancy, to cut him out of the life of his child—*if* Cody was his child.

And he was still angry the next morning, and continuing to mull over these thoughts, as he sipped his coffee.

"Are you okay?" Beth asked.

"Sure. Why?"

"Because you're gripping the handle of that mug so tight it's a wonder it hasn't snapped off in your hand."

He uncurled his fist and set the mug on the counter.

"Wilder?" she prompted.

"I guess I'm just realizing how much I missed out on, not knowing that Leighton was pregnant."

"I think, in the beginning, she didn't reach out to you because she wasn't sure she was going to keep the baby," she admitted.

He swallowed. "She considered ending her pregnancy?"

"No." Beth immediately shook her head. "*Never.* She always planned to have the baby, but she didn't know if she would keep him."

"You're talking about adoption," he realized.

Now she nodded.

"But…why?" he wondered.

"Because she wanted her baby to have a better life than she could give him as a single mother. She wanted him to have a family."

"She didn't have to be a single mother. If Leighton had told me she was pregnant, I would have offered to do the right thing."

"Because getting married for the sake of a baby is the right thing?" she asked dubiously.

"Sometimes it is," he said.

"Maybe that's why she didn't tell you," Beth remarked.

"What does that mean?" he challenged.

"I can't imagine any woman being swept off her feet by such an offer, and it definitely wouldn't have swayed my sister."

He scowled at that. "You think she would have said *no*?"

"I wouldn't presume to know how she might have responded," Beth said. "But I think the fact that she didn't tell you she was pregnant proves she didn't trust you would support her choices."

"But she trusted you?" he challenged.

"I did support her," she said.

"And yet, when she got to the point where she felt overwhelmed by her responsibilities, she brought the baby to me," he pointed out.

He was right, and that truth was like a slap to Beth's face.

She'd thought she was doing what was best for her sister. She'd offered her a sympathetic ear and a strong shoulder; she'd listened and counseled and encouraged. And all the while she'd been promising her support, she'd also been pushing her sister in the direction Beth wanted her to go. *Of course it's your choice if you want to give your baby up for adoption. But if you decide to keep him, I'll be there for you. Whatever you need. Whatever he needs.*

Leighton had been honest in expressing her reservations about working as a bartender and raising a child on her own. She'd wanted to do the best thing for her baby—to give him a real family. But Beth had pointed out that they were a family; she'd assured her that they could be everything he'd ever need. And so Leighton had been persuaded to keep her baby.

But sometime during the past four months, she'd apparently had a change of heart.

Or maybe she'd begun to suspect her sister was wrong.

Either way, there was one fact that Beth could no longer deny: it was *her* fault Cody had been left on a ranch in Montana.

"We were just talking about the big New Year's Eve party at Maverick Manor," Max said, when Beth returned to the main level after putting Cody down for his nap. "It's the fancy hotel off the highway owned by Nate Crawford—you might have seen it on your way into Rust Creek Falls."

"Isn't everything in this town owned by a Crawford?" Beth asked.

"Not quite everything," Max said. Then he winked. "At least, not yet."

Beth smiled, though she suspected he wasn't entirely joking. The Crawford patriarch struck her as a man capable of world—or at least small-town—domination.

"So what do you think?" he asked.

"About what?"

"The party."

She looked at Wilder, as if he might be able to give her a clue as to why his father was asking, but he only shrugged.

"Sounds like fun?" she said.

"Great. I'll tell Nate to add your name to the guest list."

"Oh," she said, startled by the suggestion. "I meant it would be fun for you—not for me."

"You don't like parties?" Max challenged.

"She doesn't know how to have fun," Wilder said.

And though the twinkle in his eye assured Beth that he was only teasing, the remark too closely echoed her sister's oft-repeated criticism for her to slough it off.

"That's true," she said, aware that her tone was as stiff as her smile. "So while it's thoughtful of you to invite me, I have to decline."

"Don't say no," Max protested.

But she didn't stick around to discuss the matter any further. There was no point, when she knew she wouldn't change her mind.

She instinctively headed toward the guest room, just as she'd retreated to her bedroom when she was a child, as if closing the door could shut out the taunting voices that called her names.

"Worrywart."

"Spoilsport."

"Killjoy."

"Little Miss Perfect."

Sticks and stones may break my bones...

The childhood rhyme echoed in her head as Beth reached the top of the stairs.

Maybe names didn't leave physical scars, but they did hurt. The barbs stung even more when they were tossed by her sister. For as long as she could remember, Beth had adored her little sister, but she'd also been aware that her affection wasn't returned. So she'd tried harder to be liked by her sibling, to be included in her activities, to be part of her life.

Every once in a while, Leighton would invite her into her inner circle, allow her to be included in her plans. It didn't take Beth long to realize that her sister wasn't trying to befriend her so much as she was testing her. But it wasn't in Beth's nature to go along with the crowd when what the crowd was doing was questionable, dangerous or illegal. And Leighton had stopped inviting her, further cementing her status as an outcast, widening the gap between the sisters' lives.

Wilder caught up to her in the hall, before she even reached her room.

"I'm sorry," he said.

She shook her head. "You didn't say anything that wasn't true."

"But I didn't mean it."

"Yes, you did. And it's true. Leighton's the fun sister. I'm the responsible one.

"And normally that wouldn't bother me so much, except that her latest actions have been beyond irresponsible."

"You're worried about her," Wilder guessed.

"Of course, I'm worried about her. And I'm worried about Cody. And I'm mad that she doesn't seem to be worried about Cody."

She stalked back and forth in the hall. "I mean—she just left him here without telling anyone where she was going or when she would be back," Beth continued her rant. "How could she do that? And what if something were to happen to his mom? Where would that leave him?"

"I can understand your concerns," Wilder said. "But even in such a worst-case scenario, I'm confident that Cody would be just fine."

She frowned. "How can you say that?"

"Because he'd still have his Aunt Beth," he pointed out

to her. "And she's a force to be reckoned with. Brave and strong. Loving and loyal."

Inexplicably, her eyes filled.

"Oh, crap," Wilder said. "What did I say wrong now?"

She shook her head, but she couldn't stop the tears from spilling onto her cheeks. And though Wilder looked as if he'd rather be anywhere else in that moment, he drew her close and held her while she cried.

Of course he was only trying to offer her comfort, but with her face pressed against his shirt, she couldn't help but notice how the soft flannel contrasted to his hard muscles. And that he smelled really good.

"You want to tell me now what caused you to go from spitting nails to a complete meltdown in the blink of an eye?" he asked, when her tears had finally dried up.

She shook her head again.

"You don't know?" he queried.

"I don't want to tell you," she admitted.

"Why not?"

"Because you'll think I'm ridiculous."

"I won't think you're ridiculous," he promised.

"The things you said…about me being strong and loving…they were nice."

"And?" he prompted.

"No one's ever said such nice things about me before."

"You need to get some better friends," he told her.

She managed to smile at that. "I have wonderful friends," she assured him. "But I don't tend to open up and dump my emotional baggage on them."

"So why me?" he wondered.

"I guess you're just lucky."

He chuckled at that. "Yeah, that's what my niece said when a baby was left on my doorstep. And though I was skeptical at first, I'm beginning to think maybe she was right."

In only four days, Beth had seen it—he'd not just grown more comfortable with the daily responsibilities of taking care of a baby, but he'd learned to interpret Cody's cries and anticipate his needs. She'd heard it, too, in the warmth in his voice when he talked not just to Cody but about him. Forcing Beth to acknowledge that this was one more thing her sister had lied about.

Or maybe Leighton hadn't been able to guess how he would respond to the news of her unexpected pregnancy. Maybe she really hadn't known him well enough to anticipate that he would step up.

"So...will you reconsider coming to the party?" he asked.

Beth appreciated the invitation. She was even a little tempted. She couldn't remember the last time she'd gone out to celebrate the arrival of a new year, and the idea held a certain appeal. But she had nothing appropriate in her wardrobe for a night out, and no intention of trekking into town to spend money on an outfit she'd probably never wear again. Not to mention that she had no desire to see Wilder live up to his reputation, flirting with all the pretty girls in town.

"Truthfully, I'm not keen on the idea of hanging out with a bunch of people I don't know."

"You know me and my brothers," he pointed out.

Yes, and they were all—aside from Wilder and his father—engaged or married. In other words, if she went, she'd be surrounded by happy couples. And when the clock counted down to midnight, they'd instinctively turn to their significant others to embrace and kiss, reminding her once again that she was alone in the world—as she'd always been.

"I do appreciate the invitation," she said. "But I want to stay home with Cody."

Not only was that kind of celebration much more her

speed, but she sincerely wanted to spend the time with her nephew. Because she was beginning to suspect that, if Wilder was the little boy's father, he would want Cody to stay in Rust Creek Falls, which meant that her days and nights with her nephew were numbered.

"Did you convince Beth to come to the party?" Max asked, when Wilder made his way back downstairs.

"It's not my place to try to change her mind," he said, conveniently ignoring the fact that he'd attempted to do just that.

"I'm sure if you used some of your legendary charm, she'd reconsider," his father said.

Wilder narrowed his gaze. "What are you up to?"

"I'm not up to anything," Max denied.

"Then why do you care whether or not Beth goes to the party?"

"I just think she deserves a night out," his father said.

"That's the only reason?"

"What other reason could there be?"

Wilder didn't buy his father's innocent act for a minute. "Just as long as you don't have any crazy ideas in your head about matchmaking," he said.

"Why would I waste my time when I paid good money to Vivienne Dalton to take care of that?" Max countered.

"I didn't think you'd paid her anything yet."

His father waved a hand dismissively. "You know what I mean."

"I know that you've avoided giving a direct answer to the question," Wilder pointed out.

"How's this for direct? You don't need to worry that I've got any illusions about you and our houseguest from Dallas," Max assured him. "It's obvious that Cody's aunt isn't at all your type."

"I'm glad you can see that," Wilder said, even as a part of him wondered if his father—and his own instincts—might be wrong.

When Wilder walked into the kitchen while Beth was preparing a bottle for Cody on New Year's Eve, her heart actually bumped against her ribs. Because as good as Wilder looked in his usual jeans and flannel, decked out in a suit and tie and dress boots, he was even more mouthwateringly delicious. And looking at him now, she had absolutely no difficulty understanding why her sister had been so eager to fall into bed with him.

Not that Beth would ever do the same thing.

Of course, she'd never have the chance.

Because she and Leighton were complete opposites, and though her heart might act a little crazy whenever Wilder was near, the handsome cowboy had given her absolutely no indication that the unwelcome attraction she felt was reciprocated.

Well, except for that one time, when he'd brushed the remnants of gooey marshmallow off her lip and looked at her in a way that made her feel all gooey inside. But again, that was probably only her overreaction to a casual gesture not intended to be anything else.

"You clean up good, cowboy." She kept her tone light, as if she was unaffected by his appearance and merely making an observation.

He took a moment to peruse her outfit in turn: a chunky knit sweater, black leggings and wool socks. "And you look comfortable and warm," he said, with a wink.

"Because I am," she agreed.

"It's not too late to change your mind and come with us," Max said, entering the room.

He was dressed in a similar fashion to his son, and looking at him now, Beth could easily imagine what Wilder would look like in another thirty-five years—and it was a good look.

"Hunter and Merry are staying home with Wren tonight and said they'd be happy to watch Cody if you wanted to go out," he explained.

"I don't want to go out," Beth said. "But thank you again."

"Well, Happy New Year then," Max said, nudging his son toward the door.

She wished both men a happy new year in return, then locked the door behind them and settled in for a quiet night with her nephew.

As always, the advent of a new year caused her to look back and reflect on all the wonderful things that had happened in the past twelve months—the most notable event being Cody's arrival. She wondered if Leighton was thinking about him today, too. Maybe even missing him a little.

Six days had passed since she'd left Cody at the Ambling A Ranch. Seven since Beth had arrived at her sister's apartment on Christmas Eve in eager anticipation of celebrating the holiday together. And in all that time, she hadn't heard anything from Leighton. Not a single word aside from that brief and cryptic message left by her phone.

Maybe she could understand her sister not reaching out to her—especially if Leighton didn't want to answer the questions she knew Beth would ask—but she couldn't understand her not being in communication with her friends. Or her boss. And a full week's absence from social media was unprecedented.

Beth picked up her cell now, as if she could will her sister to call, but it remained silent, the screen blank. Of course, wherever Leighton was—unless she'd left the country—it was December 31, so she was probably out celebrating. There was nothing Leighton loved more than a party. The wilder the better. And yes, it had crossed Beth's mind, when she found Wilder's name and address in her sister's apartment, that Leighton would have found his name as appealing as the rest of him.

Beth had always been attracted to a different kind of man. The kind who would prefer a simple "dinner and a movie" date over loud music and fancy cocktails in a trendy nightclub. The kind who aspired to obtain a wife and a family rather than fast cars and faster women. She wanted a simple man with simple dreams.

Which was why her attraction to Wilder wasn't just unexpected but unwelcome. Because if he was her sister's type, he was definitely *not* hers. Unfortunately that knowledge didn't stop her pulse from racing when he was near, or prevent butterflies from swirling in her belly when he smiled at her, or cool the blood that heated when he touched her.

Aside from the fact that he wasn't her type, he was quite possibly her nephew's father. And regardless of whether or not the DNA results proved he was Cody's dad, there was no denying that he'd had an intimate physical relationship with her sister. Yes, that relationship had ended a long time ago, but it still felt as if she was violating some kind of unwritten code.

Or maybe a written code, she acknowledged, as coveting thy sister's lover was undoubtedly the moral equivalent of coveting thy neighbor's spouse.

Thou shall not, she reminded herself sternly.

But even if she did covet, nothing would ever come of her desires, because Wilder would never be attracted to someone like her. His history with her sister proved that he preferred a very different kind of woman.

So really, any fantasies that played out in her head—or in her dreams—were just that. And fantasies aside, she was happy with her life. She had a great job, a nice apartment, good friends and friendly neighbors, and now she had Cody, too.

The birth of her nephew had filled her life in ways she couldn't have imagined. But now she had to face the very real possibility that, if Leighton didn't come back and the DNA test proved that Wilder was Cody's father, she could lose him.

She no longer had any doubts that the cowboy would pursue legal custody of his child. And the courts, taking into consideration the biological connection and Leighton's apparent abandonment of her child, would likely rubber-stamp his application.

Sure, Beth could put in a claim for guardianship and argue that she had a stronger bond with her nephew, who'd never even met Wilder until he was four months old. But the courts tended to favor placement of a child with a parent, and they certainly wouldn't hold it against Wilder that he'd had no contact with a child he'd known nothing about.

Even if she believed she was better equipped to deal with Cody's day-to-day needs, she couldn't deny that Wilder had a lot of family support in Montana. And though she'd had limited interactions with his siblings and their spouses, it was evident that they'd readily accepted Cody as part of the family.

So the most likely scenario was that Cody would stay in Rust Creek Falls and she would go back to Dallas, and maybe she'd get to see her nephew a few times a year. The prospect made her heart ache unbearably.

Of course, if Leighton came back to reclaim her baby and Wilder consented to her returning with him to Dallas, then the status quo of Beth's life would be restored. Or maybe Leighton would return and decide to give her relationship with the cowboy another chance—to give Cody a family. Which was what Beth wanted more than anything for her nephew, even if it meant she'd be left on the outside looking in.

But perhaps this was a lesson to her. A reminder that she needed to live her own life and let Leighton live hers. Whether or not she agreed with her sister's choices, she had to accept that they were hers to make. And if Leighton made mistakes, she would have to own them and learn from them.

And maybe it was time for Beth to make some mistakes, too. Or at least take some chances. She'd mostly given up on dating, having grown tired of putting herself out there in an effort to meet "the right guy" only to find that she didn't click with anyone. Or, when she thought she clicked, to realize she'd been duped by someone who'd only said and done the right things to get her into bed and then totally ghosted on her.

Maybe she should put herself out there again—say "yes" the next time Barry Kendrick asked her to go out with him. So what if the fifth-grade science teacher didn't make her heart race or her belly quiver? It was time to grow up and accept that those physiological reactions didn't exist outside the pages of the romance novels that she loved to read.

Except that her body's responses to Wilder Crawford proved otherwise.

Chapter Eleven

Looking around the festively decorated ballroom of Maverick Manor, it seemed to Wilder that after a lot of years and a lot of parties, they all started to look and feel the same. The glittery venues and beautiful women mixed with champagne bubbles and blurred together in his mind.

His memories of last year's celebration, being the most recent, were perhaps a little clearer. He and Leighton had been seeing each other for a few weeks by then, and he easily pictured the sparkly green dress that hugged her curves and the sexy skyscraper heels that put her mouth within easy reach of his. But the rest of the details remained fuzzy.

He knew she had pale blond hair and moss green eyes, but the image that teased his mind now was of dark hair and dark eyes. And as the features came more fully into focus, he noticed other inconsistencies: the lush mouth was a little too full, and instead of being painted glossy red, the lips were naturally pink. Naked. And somehow even more tempting.

Beth's lips.

The realization was as startling to Wilder as it was unsettling.

Scowling, he escaped to the outdoor terrace to get some air and clear his head.

Looking around at the crowd, everyone decked out in their holiday finest, it belatedly occurred to him that Beth might not have wanted to come to the party because she didn't have anything appropriate to wear. He would have been happy to take her shopping, if she'd asked, though the way she'd balked at shopping with him the last time, he wasn't surprised that she didn't. Which was too bad. He wouldn't mind seeing her in something other than the jeans or leggings and bulky sweaters she seemed to favor. Or maybe in nothing at all.

Uneasy with the direction of his thoughts—and uncomfortable outside without a coat—he returned to the gathering. After a quick stop at the bar, he stood on the periphery of the crowd and spotted his father in conversation with an older, petite blonde he didn't recognize.

Could this be the mystery woman his father had gone into Kalispell to have dinner with? Max had been uncharacteristically tight-lipped the day after his date, volunteering no details and refusing to respond to his son's questions. But whoever this woman was with the platinum curls and four-inch heels, she seemed to have Max's complete and undivided attention.

And because Wilder was watching them, he didn't notice the pretty brunette who'd sidled up to him until she spoke. "Can I buy you a drink?"

His smile was automatic as he turned. She had dark hair pinned up in some kind of fancy twist, with a few strands pulled loose to frame her heart-shaped face. Her eyes were as blue as the sapphires in her ears and sparkled with wicked promise.

She was beautiful and confident and not at all subtle about what she wanted—the type of woman who usually made his blood hum in his veins. And yet, when he looked at her, he felt nothing but a vague appreciation for her obvious attributes.

In response to her question, he held up the bottle of beer in his hand. "I've already got one."

"Then I guess you should buy me one," she said.

Even if he wasn't interested, it wasn't in his nature to be rude. So he put his hand on her back and led her to the bar, where she ordered some kind of froufrou cocktail that set him back twenty bucks. A small price to pay for a man interested in what she was obviously offering. But he wasn't that man. Not tonight.

She introduced herself as Simone and told him that she lived in Billings but had come to Rust Creek Falls to visit a friend from college who'd recently split from a longtime boyfriend. Except that the longtime boyfriend had apparently seen the error of his ways and showed up with an engagement ring in hand, leaving Simone to celebrate on her own.

"Or maybe not entirely alone," she said hopefully.

"You're never really alone in a crowd like this," he remarked, looking around for one of his brothers in the vague and futile hope someone might come to his rescue.

He caught a glimpse of Logan, snuggled up with Sarah, oblivious to the world around them. Of course, even if he managed to snag Logan's attention, his brother would never guess that Wilder wanted to be rescued.

"Is something wrong?" Simone asked, licking her lips to remove the pink sugar that had transferred from the rim of her glass.

"What?"

"You're frowning," she told him.

"Sorry." He smoothed his brow. "I guess my mind was wandering."

"Not something a woman wants to hear when she's flirting with a handsome man," she chided, stroking a long, painted fingernail down his arm.

"Sorry," he said again. "It's not you, it's me."

The warmth in those blue eyes immediately chilled. "Yeah, I've heard that one before. Too many times." She stepped back then. "Thanks for the drink."

Then she turned and walked away.

He could have called her back. He knew how to turn on the charm and, with a wink and a smile, he could have smoothed her ruffled feathers and been kissing her at the stroke of midnight.

But he didn't want her to come back. He had no interest in yet another meaningless encounter with a virtual stranger.

A movement caught the corner of his eye, and he glanced over to see his brother Knox flying his hand through the air like a makeshift plane, then tipping his fingers to dive down and spreading them apart.

Wilder lifted a brow. "Are you having fun?"

"As a matter of fact, I am," Knox said. "Because not only am I here with the sexiest woman in all of Rust Creek Falls, but I just watched my little brother—the one that no woman can apparently resist—crash and burn."

"I didn't crash and burn," he denied.

"What are you guys talking about?" Xander asked, unapologetically shoving his way into their conversation.

"Our baby brother just crashed and burned," Knox said.

"You wish," Wilder retorted.

"So the sexy brunette with the mile-long legs in the skintight dress didn't just walk away from you?" Knox challenged.

"She walked away," he confirmed. "But only because I didn't want her to stay."

Xander frowned, feigning concern. "Did you hit your head when you crashed?"

"I didn't—" Wilder huffed out a breath. "You know what? I don't care. If you want to believe I crashed and burned, fine."

His brothers exchanged a glance.

"Okay, now I'm seriously starting to worry that there's something wrong with you," Knox said.

"There's nothing wrong," Wilder assured them. "I'm just not in the mood to spend the night with a woman who doesn't mean anything to me."

"But isn't that your whole MO?" Xander asked.

"If you stop having sex with women who don't mean anything, you won't be having sex with anyone," Knox warned.

"Unless he's met a woman who could actually mean something," Xander mused thoughtfully.

"Wilder?" Knox snorted. "As if."

"If you'd focus your attention on your own woman, you might realize that she's trying to snag your attention before she waves her arm right out of its socket," he replied.

Thankfully, the distraction worked in shifting the topic of conversation, but his brothers flanked him and maneuvered him over to the big table occupied by his siblings and their partners.

"What's going on?" Knox asked, when he'd lowered himself into the vacant seat beside Gen.

"Lily was just telling us the most recent news about the mystery lover in the Abernathy diary," she said, referring to the jewel-encrusted book they'd found hidden in the floorboards shortly after moving to the Ambling A.

"Am I the only one who feels uncomfortable about reading someone's diary?" Avery wondered aloud.

"Yes," Lily said. "I mean, a person's privacy should be respected, of course, but this diary is practically a historical document. And I believe Josiah Abernathy put his innermost thoughts on paper because he expected—or maybe even hoped—that someone else would read his words someday."

"Maybe the mysterious 'W,'" Sarah chimed in.

"Plus, there are some really steamy passages," Xander noted.

"Not trashy," his wife hastened to clarify. "But definitely passionate."

"I think he really loved her," Knox said.

"Who?" Logan asked.

Knox shrugged. "Whoever 'W' is."

"Are there any clues about her identity?"

"Asks the person who didn't think we should be reading the diary," Finn noted dryly.

Avery shrugged. "But since it is being read, are there any clues?" she pressed.

"Actually, there *is* something," Lily said. "Whoever she was, she was apparently pregnant with Josiah's baby."

Avery gasped. "He had a child with his mystery lady?"

Lily shook her head. "Apparently the baby was stillborn."

"Oh." The expectant mom instinctively touched a hand to the slight curve of her belly, as if to protect her own unborn child from such a tragic fate. "That's so sad."

Lily winced. "I'm sorry. I wasn't thinking—"

Avery shook her head. "There's no need to apologize. And I am as curious as everyone else about Josiah and the history of the Ambling A."

"Well, apparently 'W' was so devastated by the loss of her child that she went crazy."

"Literally or figuratively crazy?" Sarah asked curiously.

Her friend and sister-in-law shrugged. "I can only tell you what's written in the book."

"I asked because I'd heard that Winona Cobbs apparently spent some time in an asylum after the Abernathys left town," Logan's wife explained.

"The definitely eccentric and questionably clairvoyant Winona Cobbs?"

"The one and only," Sarah confirmed.

"But I've lived in Rust Creek Falls my whole life and I've never heard so much as a whisper of a rumor that Winona Cobbs was ever pregnant," Gen said.

"She wouldn't be the first woman to keep an out-of-wedlock baby a secret," Sarah remarked. "Especially so many years ago."

"Except that Winona isn't exactly known for her ability to keep secrets," Lily commented.

"And if the diary is as old as we think, she would have been a teenager at the time," Knox chimed in.

"On the other hand, if she did lose a child, well, that might explain why she's always been a little...odd," Gen acknowledged.

The mystery was admittedly intriguing, but as Wilder had nothing to add to the conversation, he decided to abandon the party and return to the place where it all started.

Max watched his youngest son slip away from the gathering and head out alone. Though Wilder had always enjoyed a party, he wasn't surprised to see him go. His life had been turned upside down since he'd found Cody on the doorstep, and though he'd yet to acknowledge the child as his own, over the past week, Wilder's denials of paternity had become less frequent and less adamant.

Max didn't blame him for not embracing the baby with open arms, because he knew it wasn't just the responsibilities of fatherhood that Wilder found daunting. It was the memories that had been stirred up by the realization that Cody's mother had walked out on him. Just like Sheila had walked out on her children when Wilder wasn't much older than Cody was now.

Of course, his youngest son had no real recollection of Sheila leaving, but he'd grown up believing that she'd chosen a life with another man over her children. Because that was what Max had wanted him to believe. What he'd wanted all his children to believe. Because admitting the truth would mean admitting that it was his fault his six sons had grown up without their mother.

"That's gotta be one of your boys," his female companion said, following the direction of his gaze.

Max nodded. "My youngest."

"He's a lucky boy," she remarked, with a bold wink. "Because he's almost as handsome as his daddy."

He smiled, appreciating her company and her flattery.

Of course, Max had always appreciated beautiful women, and Estelle fit the bill well enough. Blond curls framed a flawless face with thickly lashed blue eyes, a pert nose and slickly painted lips. He suspected she'd paid a price to retain—or maybe even enhance—her natural attributes, but he had no objections to hair dyes or face paint or even a little nip and tuck. Not when the results were so appealing.

Though she was barely five feet tall without the skinny heels that added several inches to her height, and probably not more than ninety pounds, she would never be described as diminutive. She was bossy and opinionated and didn't know the meaning of the word *quit*.

Some eighteen months earlier, she'd sold her wedding planning business to Vivienne Dalton—the same woman he'd hired as a matchmaker for his sons, though she'd been Vivienne Shuster at the time and the business had been located in Kalispell. Then Estelle had moved down to Phoenix to work with her sister in the funeral business. Six months later, she'd decided that the Grand Canyon State wasn't for her and returned to Kalispell.

"I'm not overly fond of cowboys," she'd said at their first meeting—set up by Vivienne Dalton—at a bar in her neighborhood. "But you don't look like the kind who buys his jeans at the same place he gets feed for his horses."

"I'm not overly fond of outspoken women," he'd replied, more amused than insulted by her blunt assessment. "And you do look like the kind who has an opinion about everything and not enough sense to know when to keep it to herself."

She'd smiled then. "You going to buy me a drink?"

"You going to order something ridiculously girly?"

She asked the bartender for Jack Daniel's Single Barrel Select, straight up. He'd had the same, and they'd chatted some more while they'd sipped the smooth whiskey.

Tonight, she was drinking champagne, as most of the other guests in attendance were doing. She lifted her glass to her lips now and swallowed the last mouthful of bubbly, then opened the clasp of her handbag and frowned as she examined its contents.

"Did you lose something?" he asked.

"I keep forgetting that I don't smoke anymore," she confided.

"Smoking's a bad habit," he said.

"My doctor spent years telling me the same thing," she confided. "But it wasn't until my sister lost her husband to lung cancer that I finally managed to kick it."

He nodded, only half listening to what she was saying.

But apparently Estelle was more intuitive than he'd given her credit for, because she stopped rambling about the treatments that had taken as much of a toll on her brother-in-law as the disease and asked, "What's got you so worried about your son?"

"He's going through some stuff right now," Max answered vaguely.

"In other words, none of my business," she guessed.

"More that it's not my place to tell," he said.

"Well, then, why don't we take ourselves to my place where I'll be better able to help you forget your worries?"

Max wasn't convinced anything could make him forget his worries, but he was willing to let her try.

The house was quiet after Wilder and Max had gone.

Too quiet.

Or maybe it was the isolation of the ranch that made Beth a little uneasy.

She was a city girl born and bred, accustomed to the lights and noises of an urban setting. Here, it was so quiet she'd be able to hear crickets if the insects hadn't entered into a state of complete dormancy to survive the frigid winter season.

She turned on the television to provide some background noise. Because being alone with the baby, she found herself jumping at every creak and groan of the big old house. She wouldn't be so uneasy if there was a dog around—and wasn't having a dog a prerequisite of being a rancher?

They'd had a German shepherd named Rowdy for almost thirteen years, Wilder had confided when she'd asked him the question. But they'd had to put him down only a few months before making the move from Dallas, and Max had vowed that he'd never get another dog. Wilder didn't really believe it was true, especially considering how Max fussed over Harry and Dobby—the two dachshunds that belonged to Xander and Lily, but for now, he was without a canine companion.

And Beth was a great big fraidycat, she acknowledged to herself as she plugged in the lights of the Christmas tree to enjoy the holiday display—and because she hoped more lights would make her less likely to jump at shadows.

Wilder had told her that they always went out to cut down a tree two weeks before Christmas and took it out of the house again on New Year's Day. Which reminded her that she'd have to deal with her own holiday decorations when she got home. So maybe it was fortunate that she didn't have a real tree. If she did, it would likely be nothing more than a bare trunk surrounded by a pile of dry needles by the time she returned.

After Cody had his cereal and his bath, Beth read him a couple of the books he'd got for Christmas. She guided his fingertips over the textured pages so he could feel soft and rough, bumpy and slippery, scaly and furry. By the time she closed the cover, his eyes were drifting shut.

"Look, Cody, they're having a big party in New York City. See all the people?" She pointed to the TV screen to direct his attention.

Though she knew television wasn't recommended for babies so young, she wasn't yet ready to take him upstairs and face the reality of spending yet another New Year's Eve alone. But Cody's eyes were closed before the ball dropped in Times Square, so she finally put him in his crib and turned on the baby monitor.

When she returned to the company of the television in the family room, she scrolled through the channels until she found another station that was counting down to the New Year, this time in Chicago. She'd just started to relax on the sofa when she heard what sounded like footsteps on the porch.

She froze, straining to hear over the thundering of her heart, even as she tried to assure herself it was nothing but her own overactive imagination.

But then she heard it again. A sound like feet stomping outside the door. Definitely *not* her imagination.

It might have occurred to her that an intruder wouldn't likely make so much noise, but at the moment, the rational part of her brain didn't seem to be communicating with the rest of her.

She pressed the mute button on the remote and strained her ears. It was a click this time, like the dead bolt being released, then a creak, as if the door had opened.

She dropped the remote to grab for her cell phone, ready to dial 9-1-1 and trying not to speculate about the length of time it would take the local police to arrive at her isolated location.

"Beth?"

All the air trapped in her lungs whooshed out in a single breath as she recognized Wilder's voice. She set her phone aside and willed her heart rate to return to something approximating normal.

"In the family room," she said, picking up the remote again to unmute the television so that she could pretend his unexpected early return hadn't scared ten years off her life.

"What are you doing home already?" she asked, when he appeared in the doorway.

He shrugged. "The party was a little too noisy and crowded for my liking."

"Aren't those the usual prerequisites of a party?" she asked.

"I guess so," he acknowledged. "But tonight I just wanted to be home."

"I'm not judging," she assured him.

He glanced at the baby monitor on the table beside her. "Cody asleep?"

She nodded. "He just went down."

He checked his watch. "It's a little late for him, isn't it?"

"Yeah, but it's New Year's Eve and he wanted to watch some of the celebration in New York City with me," she explained.

One side of his mouth tipped up in a half smile that never failed to do crazy things to her insides. "He did, did he?"

"He did," she confirmed, unwilling to admit that she'd deliberately tried to keep her nephew awake because she hadn't wanted to be alone.

But now she was alone *with* Wilder, and she wasn't sure if that was better or worse.

Then he loosened his tie and opened the top button of his shirt, and she decided it was both better *and* worse.

Chapter Twelve

As Beth watched Wilder unbutton his shirt, all rational thoughts slipped from her brain, her mouth went dry and her body got warm. His fingers deftly unfastened the second button and, imagining how those strong, calloused hands might feel against her skin, she felt a quiver low in her belly.

She wondered if he would open a third button, and then a fourth, so that she could discover if his broad chest and flat stomach were as chiseled in real life as they were in her imagination. Because yes, she'd imagined and fantasized about the handsome cowboy undressed. Dreamed about him—about his naked body entwined with her own. And woken up embarrassed and ashamed to realize that she could harbor such wanton feelings for a man who'd been her sister's lover—and was very likely the father of Leighton's baby.

Beth swallowed hard and tried to quash the lustful thoughts that teased her body and her brain.

"What?" she asked, when she realized he'd spoken but she hadn't heard a single word.

"I asked if it was okay for me to hang out here with you."

"It's your house," she reminded him.

"But you've got the remote."

"That means I'm in charge?"

He smiled at her dubious tone. "At least in charge of the TV."

She handed the controller to him. "I should probably head up to bed, anyway."

"It's not even ten thirty," he pointed out, his voice tinged with amusement.

"Oh," she said, feeling foolish. Because even a killjoy like her knew that going to bed at ten thirty on New Year's Eve was beyond lame. "I guess I could stay up a little longer. But I'm going to apologize in advance."

"For what?"

"The fact that I'll probably fall asleep before the clock strikes midnight."

He gasped, feigning shock. "On New Year's Eve?"

"Cody was up three times last night," she told him. "I'm convinced, by the way he's been gnawing and drooling, that a couple of teeth will be breaking through soon."

"Is that what the book says to watch for—gnawing and drooling?"

"There isn't one book that's the authority on everything, and every baby is different," she chided. "But yes, those are generally recognized as common signs of teething."

"If you don't think you'll make it to midnight, maybe we should crack open a bottle of champagne now and toast the New Year along with Chicago," he suggested.

"Sounds good to me," she said.

He retrieved a bottle of bubbly and a couple of glasses, popping the cork with an ease that attested to experience. And didn't that immediately highlight the differences in their lifestyles, that he could make an offhand suggestion and know the fancy wine would be chilling? If she ever expressed a spontaneous desire for champagne, the spontaneity would invariably be lost as she made a hurried trip to buy it, with her fingers crossed that the local store sold it already chilled.

He could have chosen to sit anywhere. There were plenty of options in the spacious room: the love seat adjacent to the couch she occupied, one of a trio of armchairs, or even the other end of the big sofa. For some reason, he chose to sit right beside her, so close that their thighs were touching.

He handed her a flute of champagne, tapped the rim of his own glass to hers and said, "Happy Almost New Year."

"Happy Almost New Year," she echoed, and took a tentative sip of the bubbly.

The cool and crisp liquid tickled as it slid down her throat, causing an almost irresistible urge to giggle. She swallowed the urge along with another sip of champagne.

"So how does this year compare to your last New Year's Eve?" Wilder asked her.

"It's almost a carbon copy," she admitted. "But with a much better bottle of wine." And the unexpected company of a very handsome cowboy—though she wisely kept that part to herself.

"You mean you sat at home watching other people celebrate the occasion?"

"I wasn't lying when I said parties aren't really my thing."

"Why not?"

She shrugged. "I've just never felt comfortable around a lot of people. I prefer more intimate gatherings." Then, realizing how her words might be misconstrued, she hastened to clarify, "I didn't mean *intimate* intimate. I only meant that I prefer smaller groups and quieter settings."

And then, to stop herself from babbling even more, she lifted her glass to her lips again.

"Intimate should definitely involve a smaller number," he agreed, with a wink. "My preference has always been two."

She couldn't agree, because he might interpret that as flirting. And she couldn't disagree, because if she suggested "or three or four," he might think she was advertising an adventurous spirit she did not have.

"Or one," she said, deciding that was a safe option and also a truer reflection of her status.

It wasn't until his lips curved that she realized her mistake.

"You like to go it alone sometimes, Beth?"

She could really use a blast of Montana wind to cool her cheeks right now. In the absence of that, she sipped more of the chilled wine.

"I'm going to stop talking now," she decided.

His warm chuckle skimmed over her like a caress. "I didn't mean to embarrass you," he said.

"I think I embarrassed myself," she acknowledged, and was grateful when Wilder steered the conversation to more neutral topics.

They talked about books and movies and the successes or failures of books turned into movies. Then they debated the merits of favorite sports teams, with Wilder insisting that the Cowboys would win another Super Bowl before the Stars took another run at the Stanley Cup and Beth confiding that she'd rather watch the Rangers over the Mavericks any day of the week.

He shook his head. "Clearly you know nothing about basketball."

She narrowed her gaze. "What's your foundation for that claim? The fact that I prefer baseball?"

"And that watching baseball is about as exciting as watching paint dry."

"Clearly you know nothing about baseball," she told him.

"What I do know is that it's almost midnight and you're still awake," he noted, tipping the bottle to pour more champagne into her glass.

"I'm as surprised as you are," she said.

"I'm glad I didn't bore you to sleep."

"You didn't bore me at all. In fact, I quite enjoyed your company tonight."

"Who would have guessed that we could spend an evening together without sniping at one another?" he mused.

"We've spent a lot of time together over the past few days without sniping at each other," she pointed out.

"Yeah, it turns out that you're not quite as uptight as I originally thought."

"And I've been pleasantly surprised to discover that you're not as immature and irresponsible as my first impressions led me to believe."

He smiled. "There it is."

Her brows drew together. "I think I missed something."

"Because you haven't been paying attention," he chided.

"To what?"

"You've got passion and spirit, Lisbeth Ames. But—one early-morning outburst aside—I usually only see it in defense of your sister or your nephew. I'm happy to know that you're also capable of fighting back in defense of yourself."

"I thought we were trying not to fight."

"It turns out I enjoy our verbal sparring," he admitted.

"Given the choice, I'd rather be a lover than a fighter," she said.

Wilder's brows lifted. "Is that so?"

"I didn't mean—" She huffed out a breath. "I always seem to be putting my foot in my mouth around you."

"Let's see if we can find a better use for your mouth," Wilder suggested, as he set both of their champagne glasses aside.

And then he kissed her.

It wasn't a deep or passionate kiss—more a tentative exploration. And yet, when his lips brushed over hers, a jolt of arousal surged through her body, leaving hot tingles in its wake.

She lifted her eyes and saw that he was looking as shaken by the chemistry as she felt. Then his gaze shifted to her mouth, as if he maybe wanted to try that again.

Because she wanted the same thing, she took the initiative this time and leaned forward to kiss him. And he responded. His arm snaked around her waist, pulling her onto his lap so that her knees straddled his hips and her breasts tingled where they touched his chest, her nipples stiffening to tight peaks.

She pressed herself closer, relishing the feel of his rock-hard body. She slid her hands over his taut, sculpted shoulders to link them behind his head, her fingertips tangling in the ends of his hair.

He opened her mouth to deepen the kiss, exploring the sensitive inner recesses with his oh-so-talented tongue. She rocked against him, subconsciously mimicking the rhythm of mating, until he clamped his hands on her hips, stifling her moments.

"I'm going to embarrass myself if you don't stop that," he warned.

"I don't want to stop," she said. "But—"

"Shh." He brushed his lips gently over hers now. "Let's not analyze all the reasons this might be a mistake."

Then he nuzzled her throat, and the erotic scrape of his stubble against her skin made her shiver.

"But it would be, wouldn't it? Getting naked together would further complicate an already complicated situation."

"Or maybe it would simplify it," he suggested.

"How do you figure?"

"Sex is simple—the most primal and essential connection between a man and a woman," he explained, as he slid his hands under her sweater and up her torso to cup her breasts.

And the feel of those calloused palms moving over her skin was even more delicious than she'd imagined.

She moaned softly.

"I really like those noises you make when I touch you," he told her.

"Then keep touching me," she suggested.

"I don't think I can stop."

He rose to his feet then, effortlessly lifting her with him. She wrapped her legs around his waist, hooking her ankles as he carried her toward the stairs.

She felt like a fairy-tale princess in the arms of her Prince Charming.

Except that Wilder wasn't *her* anything and there was no happily-ever-after with him in her future.

But would it be so wrong to enjoy this one magical night? A stolen moment in time before the realities of the world descended upon them once more?

He carried her to the guest room, then set her on her feet beside the bed to whisk her sweater over her head and strip away her leggings.

"You, too," she said, unfastening the remaining buttons of his shirt to reveal a strong chest and rippling abs. *Definitely as chiseled as I'd imagined.* She touched her lips to his taut, warm skin, then flicked out her tongue. *And every bit as delicious.*

While she explored his chest, he discarded the rest of his clothes, then eased her onto the mattress, bracing himself over her and capturing her mouth with his again.

He seemed to know just where and how to touch her to heighten her desire, maximize her pleasure. Eager to reciprocate, she tentatively reached between their bodies to wrap her hand around his hard, velvety length. He pulsed in her hand; a groan rumbled in his chest. Emboldened by his response, she stroked her hand toward the tip, then back down again.

He unclasped her bra, releasing her breasts from the restraint of the lacy cups. Her already peaked nipples drew tighter when the cool air whispered over her skin.

He drew one of the aching tips into his mouth, tugging gently with his teeth, until she moaned and arched beneath him. His mouth moved to her other breast, affording it the same attention as his hands stroked over her body in a teasing exploration that made her quiver and yearn.

He gently parted her thighs, opening her to a more intimate investigation. His fingertips skimmed the sensitive skin of her inner thighs and traced the lacy edge of her panties, making her muscles tremble. Then his thumb brushed over the aching nub at her center, through the thin fabric barrier, making her whimper.

His mouth moved lower, skimming over her torso, then he caught the narrow band of lace at her side in his teeth and dragged it down over her hip before switching to the other side. He continued to alternate from side to side, inching her panties downward until they were dangling around one ankle. Then he spread her legs wide and lowered his head between them.

She felt the scrape of his stubble against the sensitive skin of her thighs, a surprisingly erotic sensation. When he touched her with his tongue, she gasped, shocked by the unexpected intimacy. And again, because the pleasure was more than she'd anticipated. More than she'd imagined.

He nibbled and licked, tasting and teasing, driving her ever closer to the pinnacle of pleasure. Then holding her there, right on the edge, until she was desperate for release. She could hear herself whimpering, pleading.

Stop. Please. More.

She didn't seem to know what she wanted, what she needed.

But Wilder knew, and he gave it to her. More and more,

until she couldn't take it anymore. Until she was no longer on the edge, but falling, falling, falling...

Her body was still quivering with the aftereffects of her climax when Wilder retrieved a condom from his wallet, then tore open the foil packet and covered himself. Only then did he position himself over her again, and finally bury himself between her thighs.

She wrapped herself around him, her hands gripping his shoulders, her legs anchored around his torso, pulling him even deeper inside. He began to move, and she met him thrust for thrust, urging him to find the same release he'd given her.

As their bodies merged and mated, she found her own desire escalating again. He picked up the pace, driving faster, harder, deeper. Pushing her to new and even loftier heights. But this time, when she took the plunge, he went with her.

Wilder was jolted awake—and jarred out of a tantalizingly explicit and erotic dream—by the sound of a baby crying. It took him a moment to get his bearings, for his eyes to adjust to the darkness and recognize that he was in the guest room, where he'd fallen asleep after making love with Beth.

He closed his eyes again and swore quietly as the memories washed over him.

It never should have happened.

But it had happened—and it had been amazing.

He'd always preferred the company of women who were looking for short-term companionship rather than long-term commitment. Beth was all about hearth and home right down to the marrow of her bones. She was the type of woman a man would choose to marry, and Wilder had no intention of being that man—for any woman.

But, as usual last night, he'd been thinking about his

own desires, selfishly taking what he wanted with little regard for the consequences.

And now…

A soft murmur joined the sound of the baby's cries. He realized the sounds were coming through the baby monitor on the table beside the bed and that Beth was already up and tending to Cody.

Cody.

He swore again as a fresh wave of guilt washed over him.

Barely a week earlier, he'd been reflecting on how great his life was, how lucky he was that he wasn't tied down in any kind of relationship, and how he had no interest in being saddled with a kid at this point in his life.

Because a week earlier, he hadn't known of Cody's existence. Now that he did, his intentions and interests were irrelevant. The fact was, if Cody was his child, he was going to step up and be the best father that he could be to him.

But it didn't really matter whether or not the kid was his. He should never have seduced his aunt. Because the intimacies they'd shared added a whole other layer of complications to an already complicated situation. Which, now that he thought about it, was almost exactly what she'd warned him about the night before.

Asserting his parental rights and applying for legal custody would deal a devastating blow to Beth, who'd been helping to care for her nephew since his birth.

But there was no way Wilder could let the child go. He wouldn't ever abandon his son, as his mother had abandoned hers. He wouldn't let anything matter more than his child.

But wasn't that exactly what he'd done last night?

Selfishly, and not surprisingly, he'd been thinking only

about himself. About what *he* wanted. And last night, he'd wanted Beth.

Maybe the realization had surprised him a little.

Being intimate with Beth had surprised him even more.

Despite her rigid expectations and uptight manner, she was a surprisingly passionate and gloriously uninhibited woman. And if he was the type of man who did relationships, he might be willing to take a chance with her. But he wasn't, and he couldn't.

Because everything else aside, he had a history with her sister. And yes, that was probably something he should have thought about last night before he'd removed Beth's lace panties with his teeth. It didn't matter that Leighton had made it clear she was done with him. He doubted she'd be pleased to discover that he'd picked up with her sister.

But had he picked up with her sister?

Or had last night been the beginning and end?

Frustrated that all he had were questions without answers, he pushed back the covers and gathered his discarded clothes. He dressed quickly in the dark, intending to go across the hall to help with the baby.

But he paused in the hallway, watching Beth, silhouetted by the dim light, as she tended to the baby. She continued to murmur softly, soothing the child as she dealt with the wet diaper that was likely the cause of his distress. After she'd finished with that task, she'd go downstairs to prepare a bottle to fill his tummy so that he might sleep comfortably for a few more hours.

Or Wilder could take care of that for her. He'd mixed the formula enough times now that he didn't even have to read the label anymore. But as much as they took turns with feedings and diaper changes during the day, sharing such duties in the darkness of the night felt like something else. Something more.

Like something a dad and mom might do—if they were a family.

And since he didn't even know for sure if he was Cody's dad, and she for sure wasn't his mom, it would be a mistake—even bigger than the one they'd made last night—to pretend they were a family.

So instead of offering to help, he retreated to his own room like the coward that he was.

Chapter Thirteen

"Hey, big guy." Beth crooned the words softly as she unfastened the tabs of her nephew's diaper, hoping to soothe the baby but not wake the sexy cowboy asleep across the hall. "What's going on in here?"

Cody's big blue eyes were swimming with tears, his long, dark lashes wet and spikey. But his quivering lips curved, just a little.

"I bet you're not just wet but hungry," she said, as she slid a dry diaper under his bottom. "Because you've been down for almost six hours." She stifled a yawn as she wiped his bottom. "Unfortunately, I've only slept about half that amount of time, so if you could go back to sleep without too much fuss, I'd appreciate it."

Cody shoved a fist into his mouth.

"Yes, of course, I'll give you a snack first," she promised, as she fastened the new diaper, then snapped up his diaper shirt and sleeper again. "There. That's better, isn't it?"

Cody continued to gnaw on his fist as she carried him downstairs. Though she'd only been at the ranch five full days, she'd quickly learned her way around the house in the dark—a necessary skill considering the number of times she was up and down with her nephew each night.

She blinked at the light when she opened the refrigerator to retrieve one of the bottles she'd prepared earlier. She turned on the kettle to heat the water to warm the formula, then turned it off again as she recalled Sharleesa—

a colleague from work and mother of three—mentioning that her kids all preferred a cold bottle when they were teething.

"Okay, we're going to try something different tonight," she said to Cody, uncapping the bottle and lowering the nipple toward his mouth. "Let's see what you think of this."

Cody thought it was just fine, apparently, as he latched on and immediately began sucking.

"Apparently you're not afraid to try new things," Beth mused as she headed back up the stairs again. "Which proves you inherited your mama's adventurous spirit."

As usual, thinking about Leighton led to worrying about Leighton. She wished she could adopt Wilder's philosophy and not worry about things she couldn't control, but she didn't think that would ever apply to her sister.

"I didn't make any resolutions this year," she said, continuing to talk softly to Cody. "But maybe it's not too late. Maybe this year, if I make more of an effort, your mama and I will learn to communicate better and grow closer."

Of course, if she really wanted a better relationship with Leighton, she probably shouldn't have slept with her ex, Beth acknowledged ruefully.

But maybe her sister wouldn't ever find out what she'd done. Certainly Beth had no intention of telling her, and she couldn't imagine that Wilder would volunteer the information. And since she was pretty sure their impulsive lovemaking had been the result of proximity and champagne, she was confident it wouldn't ever happen again.

And that was for the best, because when Leighton came back and saw how good Wilder was with Cody, maybe she'd decide to give their relationship another chance—to give their son a real family.

It was what Beth had always wanted for Cody. So why,

then, did the idea of her sister sharing Wilder's life—and his bed—make her heart ache?

Was it somehow possible that, over the course of only five days, she'd developed real feelings for the cowboy?

Thinking about it now, she knew it wasn't just possible but true. Because during that time, she'd had plenty of opportunities to interact with him and discover his true character.

Maybe he didn't instinctively know how to be a father, but he'd proven that he was open to learning and willing to make the effort. And though she knew he had a reputation with the ladies, since she'd been at the ranch, he appeared to have made the little boy his priority over all else.

Even tonight, when he'd gone out to celebrate the New Year with his family, he'd come home early. He'd said he wasn't in the mood for the crowds, but she suspected he'd really wanted to check on Cody. Because she knew, even if Wilder wasn't ready to admit it, that the baby had already worked his way into his heart.

There was so much more to him than the picture of the wild and aimless cowboy her sister had painted. He was undeniably the most handsome man she'd ever met, but aside from his striking good looks and mouthwatering muscles, he was intelligent and charming, insightful and compassionate. He also had a good sense of humor and a strong sense of family loyalty.

And after only five days at the Ambling A and one night in Wilder's arms, she was in serious danger of losing her heart.

"Why didn't you tell me that Cody's teeth had come in?" Wilder demanded, when he returned to the house following an early ride with his brother—and after hearing the news from his father, who'd puffed up like a proud grandpa as he delivered it.

"You didn't stick around long enough for me to say anything," Beth said, pointedly referencing his quick exit earlier that morning.

"I had to ride out with Hunter to check the fence."

"I'm sure you did." She dipped the spoon into the cereal bowl again and moved it toward the baby's mouth.

When Cody opened up, she let him swallow the cereal, then used the rubber tip of the spoon to gently pull down his lower lip and reveal the bumpy ridges of white poking through his gums so that Wilder could see what all the fuss was about.

"Look at that," he said, feeling his own chest puff up with pride, as if he was somehow responsible for the baby's milestone. "He's got teeth."

"They've still got a way to go, but now that they've broken through the gums, he should be a little less cranky," she said.

"That's good," he agreed.

Now if only he could figure out why Beth seemed so cranky this morning. Or maybe he already knew—which her next words confirmed.

"Should we talk about what happened last night?" she asked.

"If you want to," he agreed cautiously.

"What I want is for things to not be awkward between us," she said.

"Do things seem awkward to you?"

"It's hard to tell when we haven't been in the same room together for more than five minutes. Or maybe that is the tell," she decided.

"I haven't been avoiding you," he promised. "Hunter texted this morning and asked me to ride out to the eastern boundary with him."

"Why you?" she wondered aloud.

"Probably because he knew all our other brothers would be snuggled up with their wives."

"Oh." She blew out a breath. "So I may have overreacted," she acknowledged. "I'm not very good at this. I don't have a lot of experience with mornings after."

"Just say whatever it is you want to say," he suggested.

"Okay," she agreed. "I think last night was a mistake. I mean, it was great, but it shouldn't have happened. We shouldn't have...gotten carried away."

"Is that what happened? We got carried away?" he asked, wondering why her dismissal of their lovemaking bothered him when he'd arrived at the same conclusion.

"Isn't it?"

"Sure," he finally agreed. "We got carried away, it never should have happened, it won't happen again."

"Okay, then," she said.

"If that's all, I'm going to make myself a sandwich and then head back out to help my brothers fix the fence."

"Of course," she agreed.

He nodded brusquely and walked out, leaving Beth to wonder why, after he'd said everything she wanted him to say, she was so unhappy.

"What's going on with you and Beth?" Max asked the following morning, when Wilder returned to the supply shed for the box of screws Knox had left behind.

"What do you mean?" Wilder asked cautiously.

"She put on boots and a coat to go out to the barn and ask Hunter to put Cody's car seat in her vehicle."

"And?"

"Why didn't she ask you?"

He shrugged. "Maybe she figured Hunter has more experience with such things."

His father acknowledged that possibility with a slow

nod. "It would have been even easier to ask you to give her a lift into town."

"She knows I'm still working with Xander and Knox to fix the fence," Wilder told him, reminding his father of the barrier that had been destroyed when someone skidded off the road and crashed through it.

They didn't know what kind of vehicle or who was responsible, as the driver hadn't contacted Max to own up to the incident. But considering the damage to the fence and the fact that the vehicle had driven away, they suspected Butch Ferrell, who owned a jacked-up Escalade and had been known to get behind the wheel after a few too many drinks at the Ace in the Hole.

"Logan or Finn could've taken your place," Max pointed out.

"And then accused me of skipping out on the hard work." Wilder shook his head. "I don't think so."

"You'd rather skip out on spending time with your son," his father remarked with obvious disapproval. "Or maybe it's Beth that you don't want to spend time with."

"If I had a choice between fixing fence and shopping, I'd go with the fence every time," he told his father.

"Are you sure that's all it is?"

"Why do you think it's anything more?"

"Because recently it seems that every time one of you walks into a room, the other one walks out."

"You ever consider that maybe we each have our own stuff to do in different places?" he suggested, because he couldn't deny the accuracy of his father's observation.

Or that, despite Beth's claim that she didn't want things to be awkward between them, they were.

His father sighed. "I thought the two of you were finally starting to get along."

"We were. We *are*," he corrected.

"Really?" Max challenged. "Because it doesn't look like it from where I'm standing."

"There's no reason for you to worry, Dad," he said, grabbing the box of nails.

"Has Beth mentioned when she plans to go back to Dallas?" Max asked, apparently not yet ready to let his son return to his duties.

Wilder shook his head. "Not before the DNA results are in. Why? Do you suddenly have an objection to her being here?"

"I don't," his dad assured him. "We've got plenty of space, and I've eaten more home-cooked meals in the past week than in the six weeks prior to her showing up."

"Which only proves that we need to hire a cook," Wilder said. "Because she's not going to be here forever."

"But she's here now," his father pointed out.

Beth obviously hadn't thought this through.

She'd just wanted to get away from the ranch and the awkward tension with Wilder for a little while, and a quick shopping trip into town seemed the perfect excuse. But she didn't have Cody's stroller—and even if she did, she wasn't sure it would navigate the snow-covered sidewalks—and it was awkward to wear his baby carrier over her coat and it didn't fit under. Which left her with no recourse but to carry him in his car seat.

At least when she got inside the store, she was able to sit his car seat in the cart while she did her shopping. She only needed a few things, but after paying for her groceries, she was faced with the logistical problem of having to cart the baby, his diaper bag and three bags of groceries out to her vehicle.

She might have asked Natalie for help, if the woman she'd met on her first trip into town had been working, but she hadn't seen her anywhere in the store. Thankfully today's clerk—identified as Nina by another customer—anticipated her dilemma and called a stock boy to carry Beth's purchases out to her car.

After all of that, she decided she deserved a treat and headed over to Daisy's Donuts, the reputed mecca of everything sweet and delicious in Rust Creek Falls. An examination of the offerings in the display case required several minutes of careful study, leading Beth to conclude that the reputation had not been exaggerated.

An opinion that was further bolstered by her first bite of chocolate silk pie.

"Hey, stranger."

Beth glanced up as Natalie Crawford slid into the seat across from her. She lifted a hand to wave, unable to offer a verbal reply because her mouth was full.

Natalie eyed the plate in front of her. "Mmm…is that Eva's chocolate silk pie?"

Beth nodded and swallowed. "Do you want me to ask for another fork?"

The other woman shook her head regretfully. "Don't think I'm not tempted, but I'm actually here to pick up a Neapolitan cake for my mom's birthday and if I let myself indulge in two desserts today, I'll never squeeze into my favorite jeans tomorrow."

"Your call," Beth said, as she dipped her fork into her pie again.

"So what brings you into town today?" Natalie asked.

"Cabin fever," she said.

"We all suffer from a bit of that during the winter," the other woman said sympathetically.

"And since I needed an excuse to go out, I decided to pick up a few groceries to make chicken and dumplings for dinner."

"You're going to spoil Max and Wilder with all your fancy cooking," Natalie warned.

"It's the least I can do," Beth said. "And I don't really do anything else."

"I would imagine this little guy keeps you plenty busy," Natalie said, glancing at the baby in his carrier on the bench seat beside his aunt. Then she smiled. "He's watching you move that fork from your plate to your mouth and wondering why you're not sharing with him."

"Because it's a little too sweet and rich for a baby who only recently started eating cereal," Beth said, directing her explanation to Cody. But she dipped the fork into the whipped cream on top of the pie, then touched the tines to his lips so that he could have a tiny taste.

He rubbed his lips together to sample the cream, then his eyes grew wide and his feet kicked.

"I think he likes it," Natalie said.

"Apparently he's got a sweet tooth like his aunt," Beth noted.

"Or maybe two of them," the other woman said. "When did he get those?"

"Just yesterday."

"New teeth for the New Year. Speaking of which… I didn't see you at the party at Maverick Manor."

"Because I wasn't there," Beth admitted.

"Surely Max invited you?"

"He did," she confirmed. "But I opted to stay home with Cody."

"Just with Cody?" Natalie teased.

"What do you mean?"

"Wilder skipped out early, causing much speculation about where he was going and who he was going to be with," Natalie confided. "Because everyone's waiting to see if Max's matchmaker goes six-for-six, and a lot of the local girls are hoping to be the sixth lucky bride."

"Is that what passes for entertainment in Rust Creek Falls?" Beth wondered, feigning only mild interest.

"Well, we've got to do something," the other woman said. "We don't even have a movie theater in town."

She smiled at that, remembering a similar discussion she'd had with Wilder on the same topic.

"In that case, I'd put my money on Max," Beth said. "He doesn't strike me as a man who ever gives up before he gets what he wants."

"And Wilder seems equally stubborn."

"Could be," she acknowledged.

"But if you were going to throw your hat in the ring..." Natalie let her words trail off suggestively.

"Me?" Beth immediately shook her head. "I'm only here because of Cody."

"That's too bad," Natalie said, sounding disappointed.

Maybe she thought so, but Beth knew it was for the best.

By three o'clock that afternoon, Wilder was rethinking his choices. Because a trip into town to do some shopping with Beth and Cody had to be better than freezing his ass off in single-digit temperatures trying to rebuild a fence.

"We should sue Ferrell for damages," he grumbled.

Though it wasn't the cost of the materials that annoyed him so much as the inconvenience of having to make the repair—and the shirking of responsibility by the idiot driver who'd crashed through the fence.

"Good luck proving it was him," Xander said.

"I heard he took his truck to a body shop in Kalispell for repairs," Knox chimed in. "Claimed someone hit his vehicle while it was parked."

"With a two-by-four?" Wilder asked facetiously, rubbing his hands on his thighs in an effort to restore some circulation to his numb digits. "Because you can bet whoever does the repair finds splinters of wood while banging out the dents."

Yeah, he definitely should have chosen to go into town with Beth—except that he hadn't been invited.

And what was that about?

They'd had the "morning after" talk she insisted on, and he'd agreed with everything she'd said—even if he didn't really agree that the night they'd spent together had been a mistake.

So why would she be mad at him?

He was tempted to ask his brothers for their take on the situation, but that would require telling them what had happened with Beth on New Year's Eve. And though he'd never shied away from talking about his past successes with the ladies, he didn't want Beth to become the object of their crude jokes.

Unless he's met a woman who could actually mean something.

As Xander's words from the night of the party echoed in his head, Wilder found himself wondering if his brother wasn't right.

Chapter Fourteen

Late the next morning, Beth was checking her email while she waited for a fresh pot of coffee to finish brewing. She scrolled through the usual ads for sales and the junk that had managed to sneak through her spam filter. There was a note from her friend Elysia, thanking Beth for the books that she'd given to Elysia's daughter for Christmas. Attached to the message was a picture of the nine-year-old on the sofa, still in her pajamas, with an open book in her hand. The photo was captioned: "And there were still presents to be opened!"

Beth smiled, pleased that her gift had been well received. After sending a quick reply, she resumed skimming through her inbox. Her heart jolted when, a little further down on the screen, she recognized Leighton's email address with a subject line that read "Wayward Sister Checking In."

She clicked on the message.

Beth—

I bet you were starting to wonder if you'd ever hear from me again. And no doubt you're pissed about my disappearing act. I know I promised to explain, but I'm not sure I can except to say that I was living a life I never thought I wanted, and it just got to be too much. And that I'm sorry.

In case you haven't figured it out by now (although I'm sure you have), I took Cody to his dad in Montana. (And I am at least 90% certain that Wilder Crawford is his dad.)

I wish I could say I took him there because I felt guilty that I'd deprived Wilder of the opportunity to know his son, and maybe I did. The truth is, I'm not sure what I was thinking in the last few days leading up to the holiday, what compelled me to pack him up and take him so far away and then leave him behind.

Yeah, Wilder's probably pissed at me, too. And I'm going to have to face up to that when I go back to Rust Creek Falls to get Cody. You don't need to worry—he's not the type of guy to take out his anger on a woman. In fact, he's a pretty good guy, and if he decides he wants Cody to visit sometime, I wouldn't mind. It might be good for him to spend time outdoors, maybe learn to ride a horse and stuff like that.

But I'm getting way ahead of myself now—those things can be figured out later. I just wanted to let you know that we'll be home soon and then we can celebrate Christmas together the way we planned.

XO

L

Reading her sister's words, Beth's initial response was relief, then happiness and hope, followed by frustration, anger and guilt. And while she could blame Leighton's actions for most of those conflicting feelings, the guilt was entirely her own.

"Do you want some of this?"

"What?" She glanced up to see Wilder holding the carafe of freshly brewed coffee over her mug. "Oh, um, yes. Please."

He filled the cup she held out, then returned the pot to the warmer. "Are you okay?"

"Yeah. Fine." But she set the mug down again without taking a sip. "I got an email from Leighton."

The surprise on Wilder's face mirrored her own response—as did the shadow of guilt that quickly followed. "You did? When?"

"Just now."

"What does it say?"

She looked at the message again. "That she's sorry for leaving the way she did and—" She cut herself off with a shake of her head. "Why don't you read it yourself?"

He took the cell from her hand and dropped his gaze to the screen.

She watched him as he scanned her sister's words, noting the flex of a muscle as he tightened his jaw—the only outward indication of any emotion, though she couldn't begin to decipher what that emotion was.

Then he handed the phone back to her. "So she's on her way back here to get Cody," he noted. "And apparently she expects me to just hand him over to her, despite the way she abandoned him."

"She is his mother," Beth pointed out.

"She abandoned him," he said again, his tone implacable.

"So...what are you planning to do?"

He swallowed a mouthful of coffee as he considered his response.

"I'll apply for custody," he decided. "I'll call Maggie right now and make an appointment to get the paperwork started."

She remembered him mentioning that he'd borrowed the crib from Maggie and Jesse, but she hadn't known the woman was a lawyer. "You don't even know for sure that you're his father," Beth reminded him gently.

"Do you really doubt it?" he challenged.

No, she didn't. Not anymore. But if she admitted as much, she might as well go back to Dallas, leaving her nephew with his dad. And maybe that was what she should do.

"I thought we agreed that no decisions would be made until we had the results of the DNA test."

"Well, if Leighton's on her way back, it doesn't really matter what you think," he pointed out. "It's between me and her and has nothing to do with you."

Though the words felt like a physical blow, she knew Wilder hadn't meant to be cruel. He was only speaking the truth as he saw it.

What really hurt was that he was right.

Any and all issues concerning Cody were for the little boy's parents to figure out.

It didn't matter that she'd dropped everything to drive halfway across the country. It didn't matter that she'd been the one helping Wilder care for Cody these past eight days. None of that mattered because he wasn't her child.

She was only a supporting player in this drama her sister had planned, and it was time for her to exit stage right.

Wilder knew his unthinking remark had hurt Beth. And as he watched her walk out of the room, he acknowledged that he might have chosen his words more carefully. Or maybe he'd wanted to put some distance between them. Because it had become increasingly evident to Wilder over the past several days that his feelings about the situation with Cody were being clouded by his feelings for Cody's aunt.

And if he was smart, he would stay where he was and maintain the distance.

Instead, he followed her path up the stairs and found her in the guest room, stuffing clothes into a duffel bag.

"What are you doing?"

"I assume that's a rhetorical question," she said, as she struggled with the zipper.

"Why are you packing, Beth?"

"Because I think it would be best for everyone if I was gone before my sister got here."

"Even for your nephew?" he challenged.

"You've proven you're more than capable of taking care of Cody."

"While I appreciate the vote of confidence, I'd argue that part of taking care of him is ensuring that he feels comfortable and secure," he said. "And I'm not sure that being abandoned by his aunt—barely more than a week after being abandoned by his mother—would do much in that regard."

"I would never abandon him," Beth said fiercely.

"You came here with the intention of taking him back to Dallas, and now you're preparing to leave without him—what would you call it?"

"Getting out of the way so that what happened between us won't be an obstacle to Cody's parents getting back together," she told him.

His brows drew together then. "Is that what you want?"

"I want what's best for Cody," she said, refusing to look at him.

"Me and Leighton together would *not* be best for Cody. And I can assure you, there is absolutely zero chance of that ever happening, anyway."

She swallowed. "Please don't say that. Don't close the door on—"

"Zero," he said again, his tone gentle but firm. "Because for me and Leighton to get back together, we would have had to be together in the first place."

She frowned at that. "You're saying you weren't together?"

"We had some good times and we had sex," he acknowledged bluntly.

"Oh."

"I'm not proud of it, but I'm not going to lie and pretend it was more than it was."

"I'm in no position to judge," she acknowledged. "I fell into bed with you, too, with no expectations of happily-ever-after…or even a kiss the morning after."

His gaze slid away. "I left your bed because I heard you talking to Cody over the baby monitor, saying you needed to get some sleep."

"How very considerate of you," she noted, her tone just a little bit cool.

"And maybe I didn't want to deal with my father's questions, if he found me leaving your room in the early hours of morning."

"Or my questions," she guessed.

"*You* told *me* it was a mistake," he reminded her.

"Because it was," she said again.

"So why are you giving me grief about it now?"

"Because I wanted you to say that it wasn't."

She looked as surprised by the blurted revelation as he felt.

"Beth," he began, then faltered.

She closed her eyes and sighed. "Sorry. Forget I said that."

"I'm not sure I even understand what you said," he admitted. "Are you saying that it *wasn't* a mistake?"

"No, it was," she said. "Of course, it was. I mean, you have a history with my sister—even if it was brief and apparently insignificant. And what happened between us… it was just two lonely people finding comfort together."

"Comfort?" he echoed, torn between insult and amusement. "When your body was shuddering with the aftereffects of multiple orgasms and you were panting my name, that was because you were feeling…comforted?"

Beth glanced away, her cheeks flushed with color. "It

doesn't matter," she decided. "We agreed it shouldn't have happened."

"Did we?" he asked.

But before she could answer, he lowered his mouth to hers.

There was no hesitation in his kiss this time. This was no tentative exploration but an insistent demand.

And she responded. She couldn't help herself. The whole time she'd been packing, she'd been recounting all the reasons that getting tangled up with Wilder was a bad idea. But somehow, with his mouth moving over hers, those reasons didn't matter. Nothing mattered but the way she felt when she was in his arms.

Her lips parted to allow him to deepen the kiss; their tongues danced in a slow and seductive rhythm that made her heart pound and her body yearn. And oh, how she yearned to experience the thrill and satisfaction of his lovemaking again.

Except that what they'd shared wasn't lovemaking but sex—a purely physical coupling with no emotional attachment required or desired. And Beth wasn't very good at keeping her emotions detached. Her feelings for Wilder were already stronger and deeper than she was willing to acknowledge.

She eased her lips from his, reluctant but determined. "Didn't we agree that what happened before was a mistake?"

"We agreed that *you said* it was a mistake," he said. "But I think you're trying to convince yourself of that so it won't happen again."

"Of course, it won't happen again."

"Because you're not attracted to me?" he challenged.

Before she could respond to that, he lifted a hand to tuck a stray hair behind her ear, skimming his fingertip over the shell of her ear, making her tremble. He smiled, letting her know that her physical reaction had not gone unnoticed, so that if she tried to claim she wasn't attracted to him, he'd know she was lying.

"Because it wouldn't be smart," she said instead.

"Attraction is rarely based on logic," he said. "And I'm very definitely attracted to you, Beth."

She swallowed. "You are?"

"After the night we spent together, how can you even ask that question?"

"We had sex—once," she reminded him. "We didn't spend the night together."

"And that's my fault," he acknowledged. "I snuck out of your bed because I wanted to stay. Because I wanted more."

"You wanted more?" she asked, doubt and hope warring inside her.

"But I don't know that I'm capable of anything more," he confided. "And you're the kind of woman who deserves a lot more. You deserve to be loved—and I don't do love. I don't know that I can."

She sighed. "So where does that leave us?"

"I don't know. But I'd like to try to figure it out."

"This really is complicated, isn't it?"

He nodded. "And likely to get even more complicated when Leighton shows up."

"That's why I think I should go," she told him.

"Even if I want you to stay?" And then, before she could reply to that, he played his trump card: "Even if Cody wants you to stay?"

She huffed out a breath. "You fight dirty."

"I fight to win," he said, unapologetic.

"Leighton will fight back," she warned.

"Are you worried that you'll get caught in the crossfire?"

She shook her head. "I can take care of myself."

"I don't doubt it," he said sincerely. "You're one of the strongest women I've ever known."

She was taken aback by his matter-of-fact tone. "You really think so?"

"I do," he confirmed. "You are fierce and formidable."

"I think you've got me mixed up with someone else."

He shook his head. "*You* are an amazing woman, Beth Ames."

And the way he said it, the sincerity in his voice, almost made her believe it.

But if he truly believed it, why couldn't he love her? Was he truly incapable of falling in love, as he believed? Or was she not worthy of his love? And why was she even thinking about love after one night with a man she'd known for barely more than a week?

"You're just trying to sweet-talk me into staying so you won't have to do the middle-of-the-night feedings," she said, in an attempt to ease the seriousness of the moment.

"If you stay, I'll happily do the middle-of-the-night feedings," he promised.

"Okay," she finally relented. "I'll stay."

Beth was folding a load of laundry as she listened to Wilder read to Cody. Hearing the simple story of *Goodnight Moon* in the cowboy's deep voice, watching him point out the list of items in the great green room, warmed something deep inside her.

The ring of her cell came between "goodnight kittens" and "goodnight mittens," and though she didn't recognize the number, she connected the call immediately so the ringing wouldn't disturb the story.

"Hello?"

"Is this Lisbeth Ames?"

It wasn't until she heard the male voice and registered a

quick stab of disappointment that she realized she'd been hoping it might be her sister calling.

"Yes," she acknowledged, bracing herself for a sales pitch.

"Are you related to Leighton Ames?" the caller asked, surprising her again.

"Who is this?" she demanded.

"This is Sheriff Burke from Clearwater County," he said. "I'm afraid I've got some bad news."

"Clearwater County?" she echoed, preferring to latch onto that detail rather than contemplate the possibility of "bad news." "I'm sorry—I don't even know where that is."

"It's in Idaho, ma'am," he said patiently, as if giving her a moment to catch up. "I'm calling because there's been an accident and—"

"What kind of accident?" she interjected, suddenly chilled to the bone recalling that it had been the sheriff who showed up at the door when her parents were killed. "Has something happened to my sister?"

"Her car spun out on Harbinger Road and slid down an embankment."

"Ohmygod. Was she hurt? Is she at the hospital?"

"I'm sorry, Ms. Ames, but your sister suffered traumatic injuries in the crash and—" He paused to clear his throat. "She didn't make it."

"I don't understand, Sheriff. What do you mean?" she asked, her brain refusing to acknowledge and accept the meaning of his words.

If he was trying to tell her that her sister hadn't yet made it back to the Ambling A, she knew that already, because she was here and Leighton clearly wasn't.

"She emailed to tell me that she was on her way to Rust Creek Falls, to pick up Cody," Beth said, eager for him to understand how important it was that Leighton keep her promise. "He's only four and a half months old and he misses her like crazy."

"I'm sorry," the sheriff said again, sounding weary.

"Don't say you're sorry," Beth snapped at him. "Tell me when she's going to be here."

"Beth." She started at the sound of Wilder's voice, gentle but firm. "Give me the phone."

She shook her head, her fingers instinctively tightening on the device, desperately maintaining her grasp on this tenuous connection to the man who was talking to her about Leighton, wanting him to explain why her sister was late.

"Cody's ready for his nap," Wilder said. "Why don't you put him down while I talk to the sheriff?"

It sounded like a reasonable request. It made sense to her. Unlike the gibberish spouted by the sheriff.

And then Wilder cleverly shifted the sleepy baby into her arms, forcing her to relinquish her grip on the phone.

She started out of the room while he took over the call, introducing himself as a family friend.

As Beth carried her nephew up the stairs, the sheriff's words continued to echo in her head, but they still didn't make any sense to her.

Accident…injuries…sorry.

She was supposed to put Cody in his crib, so that he could sleep, but for some reason, she couldn't let him go. Instead, she lowered herself into the rocking chair and snuggled him close.

The baby rubbed his face against her shoulder—a telltale indicator that he was fighting sleep. She touched her lips to the top of his head as she rocked him gently, and his eyes drifted shut.

A few minutes later, she heard the slow, steady rhythm of Wilder's footsteps on the stairs. Then he appeared in the doorway, where he remained for a long moment as if uncertain what to say or do, before crossing the room and gently removing the sleeping baby from her arms.

When Cody was settled in his crib, Wilder returned to crouch by the rocking chair.

"Hey," he said.

She couldn't respond. Her throat was too tight for any words to squeeze through. He lifted his hands to cup her face, his thumbs brushing away tears she hadn't realized she was crying.

He straightened up again, lifting her from the chair as he did so, then taking the seat and settling her in his lap, cuddling her as she'd cuddled Cody.

She wanted to protest that she was too big to be held like a baby, but it felt good to be in his arms. As the strength and warmth of his embrace penetrated the ice that had encased her body, she began to tremble.

He tightened his hold as silent tears continued to spill down her cheeks. But he didn't say anything, because what was there to say?

"I want to wake up and discover it was only a bad dream, that there was no phone call from the sheriff of—" she sighed "—where did he say he was from?"

"Clearwater County."

"Do you think it's possible they made a mistake?" she asked, grasping for any explanation other than the one she knew in her heart to be true. "Maybe Leighton's car was stolen and—"

"She identified herself to the paramedics when they first arrived on scene," Wilder said. "And the sheriff confirmed that she had a constellation tattoo."

"But Leighton doesn't have a tattoo," Beth said.

"Actually, she does," he told her, a reminder that he'd been intimately acquainted with her sister's naked body. "The Leo constellation, in the middle of her back, between her shoulder blades."

"Oh." Leo was her sister's Zodiac sign. "So it really was her? She really is…gone?"

He nodded. "I'm sorry, Beth."

She was sorry, too. And sad and angry and filled with so many more emotions that she couldn't begin to identify.

But somehow she felt empty, too.

Her sister was gone.

Not on a whim.

Not for a while.

Forever.

"I need to make arrangements," she realized. "But I have no idea where to begin, what she'd want."

She was silent for a minute, trying to focus through the grief to think. "Her friends are in Dallas. Our parents are buried there."

And suddenly the answer was obvious: "I have to go home."

Chapter Fifteen

Wilder must have told his family about the call from the sheriff and Beth's plan to return to Texas to arrange her sister's funeral, because the next morning, when she was packing her car, they were all there.

She had tears in her eyes as she said goodbye to Wilder's brothers and sisters-in-law, present and future. She tried to return Avery's jacket, but the expectant mom told her to hold onto it for the journey home, since she wouldn't be able to wear it for the next few months anyway.

Everyone took turns hugging her, expressing their condolences, and promising to see her again soon. Obviously they were assuming she'd bring Cody back to visit. Or maybe she'd be the one coming back to visit Cody, if Wilder followed through on his plan to apply for legal custody of the baby after he had the results of the DNA test.

Over the past ten days, he'd proven that he was more than capable of being the father Cody needed. Equally important, at least from her perspective, was the support of his family. And Beth knew her nephew would be lucky to be part of the close-knit and loving Crawford family.

But she couldn't think about that now. She'd barely processed losing her sister—she couldn't bear to consider that her nephew might be taken from her, too.

It had been a long time since she'd been part of a family. Since the death of their parents almost ten years earlier, Beth and Leighton had only had one another to rely on. Though she'd hoped that reality would bring them closer, there remained a distance that she hadn't been able to breach. And now she never would.

She wished her sister had called instead of emailing. She would have liked to have spoken to her one last time. To tell her that she loved her, no matter what.

"Damn, it's quiet in here," Max remarked, when he entered the house at the end of the day.

Wilder nodded. "I thought the same thing when I came in."

"And there's nothing cooking in the oven for dinner, is there?"

"Not unless you put something in there. And if you did, you forgot to turn on the heat."

Max shook his head. "You want to go to the Ace to grab a burger?"

"Not really," Wilder admitted.

"You have to eat."

"I'm not feeling very sociable," he said. Truthfully, he wasn't feeling very hungry, either.

"Want to tell me what you are feeling?" Max prompted.

"Really? You want me to talk about my feelings?" Wilder asked skeptically.

His father shrugged. "I know I'm probably not your first choice of confidant, but I'm the only one left here."

And it was a testament to how raw his emotions were that Wilder found himself opening up. "I'm mad at her," he admitted.

"Who? Beth?"

"Leighton."

"Well, there's no point in being angry with a dead woman," Max said bluntly.

"I know," he acknowledged. "And yet—I can't deny that's how I feel."

"Why are you mad at her?"

"Where to begin?"

"At the beginning?" his father suggested.

He sighed. "Okay, I'm mad that she never even reached out to tell me that she was pregnant."

"Understandable," Max agreed.

"And then, after not telling me that she was pregnant and not telling me she had a baby, she just drops him at my door and expects me to take care of him."

"That's one way to look at it," his father allowed. "Another is that she trusted you to take care of him."

Wilder just shook his head. "I don't think I'll ever understand how a woman who supposedly loves her child could walk away from him."

There was a long silence as his father considered his response—or maybe he, too, was thinking of another woman who'd done the same thing.

"Are we still talking about Leighton?" Max asked.

"Of course," Wilder said.

Because he and his brothers had learned a long time ago that asking questions about their mother only resulted in upsetting their father.

"Not every woman is cut out to be a mother," Max said now.

"So why would she assume that I could do any better at parenting? And if she needed a break, why didn't she leave Cody with his aunt? Anyone with eyes can see how much she dotes on the little guy."

"You have enough siblings to know that those relationships are never simple," his father pointed out.

"It just doesn't make any sense to me," Wilder told him.

"Is that all?"

"What do you mean?"

"I think you need to consider why you're as outraged

on Beth's behalf as you are about everything else," Max suggested.

"And why do you think that is?" he asked, because it was apparent his father had already arrived at his own conclusions.

So he was more than a little surprised when Max shook his head and said, "That's something you need to figure out for yourself."

When Beth got back to Dallas, she drove straight to the funeral home. After she'd signed the paperwork and paid the bill—which pretty much depleted her savings account—she automatically turned her vehicle in the direction of her condo.

Only as she was getting Cody ready for bed did it occur to her that he might have been more comfortable in his crib at home rather than the portable playpen he slept in when he stayed with her. But she couldn't go to her sister's apartment. Not tonight. Not knowing that Leighton was never coming home again.

She blinked back the tears that burned her eyes as she snuggled with Cody on the sofa in the living room. She didn't know if he sensed her tension or if he'd spent too many hours in his car seat over the past two days, but he seemed as wired as she felt. Though it was well past his bedtime, his eyes remained stubbornly open and fixed on her.

"I don't know what to say to you," she admitted. "How to explain what I don't understand myself. But what I can tell you, with absolute certainty, is that your mama loved you. She might have been uncertain about a lot of things, but there's no doubt she loved you with her whole heart."

Cody couldn't possibly make any sense of what she was saying, but perhaps he understood that she needed him as much as he needed her. He laid his head on her shoulder, rubbing his cheek against her shirt as he snuggled in. He exhaled a shuddery sigh, his breath warm against her throat.

By the time she finally got him settled and crawled into her own bed, she was completely drained—physically and emotionally—but sleep eluded her. She couldn't help wondering what she might have done differently so that her sister might have made different choices along the line. Or even just one different choice so that she wouldn't have been behind the wheel on that icy patch of an unfamiliar road so far away from home.

Logically, she knew it wasn't her fault. Leighton had always made her own choices, and quite often risky ones. But now, because of her choices, Cody was going to grow up without his mother.

She would have to talk to Wilder about his plans, but since receiving the call from the sheriff, she'd been focused on doing what she needed to do for her sister. There would be plenty of time, after Leighton was finally laid to rest, to worry about custody of her nephew.

But she already knew in her heart that she wouldn't fight Wilder if he decided that he wanted to raise Cody on the Ambling A. Not just because that was a fight she knew she wouldn't win, but because she knew that Cody needed a father—and Wilder deserved the opportunity to raise his son.

Ranching was both exhausting and satisfying, and it wasn't often that the activity in Max's mind overruled the weariness of his body. But tonight, he couldn't stop thinking about the conversation he'd had with Wilder, the questions his son had asked about his mother—without admitting that he was asking about Sheila.

Max rarely let himself question the choices he'd made

in his life, but he had doubts now and they were keeping him awake when he really needed to sleep.

Had he done his kids a disservice by letting them believe their mother had chosen to walk away from them, choosing her lover over her family?

He'd been so hurt to learn of her affair. Furious with Sheila, devastated by her betrayal, he'd lashed out at her. She'd chosen someone else over him, and all he could think about was hurting her the way she'd hurt him.

And Logan, Hunter, Xander, Finn, Knox and Wilder had all been casualties in the battle between the two people who should have put their children's needs above all else.

Love truly was a double-edged sword, and his children had been cut deeply. Thankfully, time—and love—had healed their wounds. Of course, Max liked to think that his decision to bring them to Rust Creek Falls for a fresh start had played a part, too. And for his five oldest sons, it had.

But Wilder was still guarding his heart. Not that anyone who didn't know him as well as his father would see it. To the rest of the world, he was just another cowboy blessed with effortless charm and a cocky grin. Only Max knew how much hurt hid behind his smile and why he didn't let anyone get too close.

Watching his youngest son with his son had given Max hope that Wilder's shields were starting to come down. No matter how much he tried to hold back, he couldn't resist responding to the child's sweetness and innocence.

The child's aunt had made a connection with the reluctant daddy, too. And not the kind of superficial connection that Wilder was famous for, but something real and deep and meaningful. But now Beth was gone, and Cody with her, and Wilder's defenses weren't just back in place but actively being reinforced.

Which left Max with no choice. He was going to have

to tell him the truth. He was going to have to fess up to all his sons.

But he had to start with Wilder.

Wilder stumbled into the kitchen on a mission for one thing: coffee. He'd slept like crap for the past two nights—and no, he wasn't blind to the fact that was the same number of nights that Beth and Cody had been gone.

Not surprisingly, his father was there before him, sitting at the table with a steaming mug of coffee in his hands. Max waited until Wilder had poured himself a mug and taken a long swallow before he spoke.

"We need to talk."

"Can it wait?" Wilder asked. "I promised to ride out with Logan today. He thinks there've been coyotes prowling around the northern boundary."

"No, it can't wait," his father said. "It's already waited too long."

Wilder's brows rose in response to the cryptic comment. "Okay…so what is it that you think we need to talk about?"

"I'm worried about you," Max said. "That you've closed yourself off from the possibility of finding love."

"Seriously? That's what you want to talk about right now? Didn't we discuss enough touchy-feely stuff the other day?"

"This is important," his father insisted.

"I know my brothers all falling in love has created some kind of wedding fever, but just because I'm not in a hurry to follow in their footsteps doesn't mean I've closed myself off," he said.

"This has nothing to do with your brothers," Max told him. "Don't get me wrong—I'm overjoyed with the recent and future additions to our family, but right now I'm focused on you."

"Well, you don't need to focus on me," he said. "I'm fine. I'm happy. Life is good."

"So why did you let Beth take Cody away just when you were finally starting to connect with him?"

Wilder frowned. "I let Beth take Cody because she was going home to bury her sister—Cody's mother—and that little boy is the only family she has left."

"That little boy is your family, too."

"Did the DNA results come when I wasn't here?"

"I don't need a piece of paper to know Cody's your son," his father insisted.

"Well, I promised Beth that no decisions would be made about Cody's future until we had the results. So if we're done here, I'm going to—"

"We're not done." Max scrubbed his hands over his face and sighed wearily. "Not even close."

Wilder refilled his mug, because something in his dad's demeanor warned him that he was going to need it.

"I know Cody's situation struck a nerve with you because you think he was abandoned the same way you were abandoned."

"The coincidence is hard to ignore," he acknowledged.

"Except that your mother didn't abandon you."

Wilder wished the caffeine would kick-start his tired body and sluggish brain so that he could keep up with his father's thought processes. "One day she was there and the next day she was gone—what would you call it?"

"She didn't leave you and your brothers...she left me."

"She left *all of us*."

Max shook his head. "She planned to find a place of her own and then she was going to move out and take you kids with her."

Wilder swallowed another mouthful of coffee. "And yet that never happened."

"No," his father agreed. "I asked her not to go. I didn't

understand why she was so unhappy in our marriage, but I offered to go to marriage counseling. I promised to change.

"But she knew me better than I knew myself," Max acknowledged. "She called my bluff. We had one session with a couples' therapist and it was a complete waste of time."

"I can only imagine," Wilder said dryly.

"I was the same man she claimed to have fallen in love with, so I didn't understand what had changed, why she'd fallen out of love with me.

"I blamed her. She'd grown up out East, living a life of wealth and privilege. And while we were well enough off, she didn't know how hard I needed to work to ensure the ranch remained successful." His father stared into the bottom of his empty coffee mug. "But it was my fault. I wasn't a very good husband. I was so busy working the ranch, I didn't think about the fact that she was alone in the house taking care of six kids. I only cared that she was there for me when I came in at the end of the day.

"When your four oldest brothers went off to school, she started taking you and Knox into town for a story time program at the library. She said it would help you both develop social skills and make friends, but it was Sheila who met someone.

"Every week, after story time, she'd stop by the little café next door. That's where she met him. He was the owner of the café, and they became friends—at least that's what she told me. But over time, their friendship grew into love."

Wilder didn't know how to respond to any of this. He could only imagine how distraught Max had been to discover that his wife was in love with another man.

"And she told me that she couldn't stay married to me when she was in love with someone else."

In his father's words, Wilder heard not just bitterness

and anger but the heartache that remained after so many years. Because while no one would ever deny that Maximilian Crawford could be a real son of a bitch, there was also no doubting that he'd deeply and sincerely loved his wife.

"So I told her she was free to go," his dad confided now. "But no way in hell was she taking my sons."

"And she chose her lover over her family," Wilder concluded.

But Max shook his head. "She said that she loved him, but she would never love anyone more than her children."

"But she left," he said again.

"She left," his father confirmed. "Because I told her to get out. I sent her away."

"Why?"

Max pushed away from the table to refill his mug of coffee. "Because I loved her and she didn't love me back. Because I was selfish and angry and hurt. Because I wanted to hurt her the way she'd hurt me."

"Why didn't you ever tell us this before?" he asked, when his father was seated at the table again.

"Because I was afraid, if you boys knew the truth…"

"If we knew the truth *what*?" Wilder pressed.

"I was afraid you'd blame me," Max acknowledged. "And you should—because it was my fault. Even when I sent her away, I knew I was acting out of anger and spite and that I'd probably regret the things I said and did. But I always thought there'd be a chance to make things right."

"Then she died," Wilder said. Not that he remembered anything from that time, but he'd been told about her sudden passing soon after the divorce papers were signed.

His father nodded. "Then she died—and it was too late to undo what I'd done. And what was the point in telling you the truth then?"

"What was the point?" he asked incredulously. "Maybe

the point was that we'd know the truth rather than thinking she didn't want us."

"You're right," his dad agreed. "But it was hard enough, living with my own guilt. I couldn't bear having to live with my sons' anger and hate."

"You should have told us," Wilder said.

Max nodded again. "I've had plenty of time to think about the choices I made," he confided. "To regret the things I said and did. It was my fault she left. My fault you grew up without a mom." He looked up then, pinning Wilder with his gaze. "My fault you haven't let yourself open your heart because you don't trust a woman to stick around."

"I know you like to think you can control everything, Dad," Wilder said dryly, "but not even you can make me fall in love or not fall in love."

Max's expression wasn't unsympathetic as he shook his head. "And you're so determined to keep your heart closed off, you can't even see that you've already fallen."

Chapter Sixteen

Wilder stood on the porch and watched the white van disappear down the driveway. Only when it was gone from sight did he turn his attention to the envelope with the purple logo of the DNA Testing Center in the upper left corner.

This was it: the moment of truth.

When he opened the flap and read the results, he would know for certain that he was Cody's father—or that he wasn't. There would be no more questions or uncertainty.

He'd been waiting for this moment for twelve days, anxious and impatient for the knowledge he finally held in his hand.

So why was he suddenly so apprehensive?

Was he afraid that the results would confirm he was the little boy's father?

Certainly, when Hunter had first read Leighton's note aloud, Wilder had been blindsided by her accusation. He hadn't wanted to believe it, because if it was true, his life would change in ways he wasn't ready for it to change.

But somehow, over the span of less than two weeks with Cody, he'd realized that he was ready for it to change. Maybe, as Beth suggested, he was even ready to embrace fatherhood not as an obligation but an opportunity.

And now he didn't want that opportunity to be taken away. He didn't want to discover that there was no biological link between him and the little boy who'd already taken hold of his heart.

He was still angry with Leighton for abandoning her child. And now that she was gone, he'd never get answers to all the questions he had. But if it turned out that Cody was his child, too, he would forever be grateful to her for giving him the chance to be the little boy's father.

But what about Beth? What would the paternity results mean for her relationship with her nephew?

She would always be Cody's aunt, but as she'd pointed out to Wilder on her first day at the Ambling A, her life was in Dallas. And if he was Cody's father, he'd want to raise him here, in Rust Creek Falls.

But maybe—

He shook his head, dismissing the thought before it had a chance to fully form. There was no point in speculating about possibilities or imagining happy endings that he knew weren't in his future. Because she was a woman who deserved a lot more than he was capable of giving. She deserved love, and he didn't do love.

Except that he did love Cody. And the way his mind and heart had been preoccupied with missing Beth, he suspected that he was starting to fall for her, too.

Starting? A voice mocked inside his head.

He ignored the voice and tore open the flap of the envelope.

His fingers trembled as he pulled out the single sheet of paper.

"DNA Test Result" was printed in bold letters at the top. Beneath it was a chart with columns of numbers that didn't mean anything to him. He scrolled further down and finally found what he was looking for: Probability of Paternity.

He didn't realize he was crying until the numbers blurred in front of his eyes.

Blinking away the tears, he refolded the page and slid it back into the envelope.

* * *

The whole time that Beth was in Rust Creek Falls, she'd looked forward to the day that she could take Cody home. At no time had she imagined that it would be for her sister's funeral.

Four days after that fateful call from the sheriff of Clearwater County, her head and her heart were still reeling from the tragic and premature death of her sister. But as much as she grieved for Leighton, she grieved even more for Leighton's baby.

But she pushed those heavy thoughts to the back of her mind for another day. Today was about Leighton, and Beth was trying to focus on celebrating her sister's life rather than mourning her death. Thinking about what would happen next—

No, she couldn't do it.

One day at a time.

That was her new motto, and today was all she could handle right now. Or maybe more than she could handle. But she would get through it, because she had no other option.

You're one of the strongest women I've ever known... fierce and formidable.

Though she'd doubted the veracity of Wilder's words when he'd spoken them to her, she called on them to sustain her now. Because she knew she was going to need every ounce of that purported strength today.

Though Cody was too young to understand what was happening, she took him to the funeral home for the early visitation. She believed it was important for him to be there, to have a last chance to say goodbye. He'd held up pretty well. It was Beth who'd cried like a baby when she put Cody's Christmas gift to his mom—the still-wrapped "Mommy" ornament—in Leighton's hand inside the coffin.

But then she'd pulled herself together, dabbed some

concealer on the dark circles under her eyes, swiped some mascara over her lashes and slicked some gloss on her lips. Not because she cared how she looked, but because she could hear the echo of her sister's voice telling her that she should care how she looked, and she knew Leighton would appreciate that she'd made the effort.

After the first visitation was over, Beth took Cody back to her condo. Moira Owen—her neighbor across the hall—had offered to watch him for the afternoon, and she was grateful for the help. Though Moira had no kids of her own, her job as an auditor for a multinational corporation meant she was a stickler for details, and Beth knew her neighbor would ensure that the baby was fed and played with and read to and put down for a nap precisely on schedule.

As for the details of her own life, she'd already been in contact with her principal, and Rebecca had told her to take whatever time she needed to get Cody settled. Beth appreciated the offer and understanding, but she wanted to get back to the comfort of her own routines as soon as possible. She needed to be busy so she wouldn't dwell on the loss of her sister—or think about Wilder.

In the three days since she'd left Rust Creek Falls, she hadn't heard a single word from him. Well, aside from the OK he'd sent in reply to her text message telling him that she and Cody had arrived safely in Dallas.

It had now been thirteen days since the cheek swabs were sent off to the lab, and she expected that he'd have the results by now. But if he did, he hadn't shared them with her.

One day at a time, she reminded herself, as she returned to the funeral home to greet those who'd come to remember her sister. Several gathered in groups, sharing stories and memories and offering comfort to one another. Beth didn't know most of them—more proof that she'd existed on the periphery of Leighton's life. And though she would always regret that they hadn't been closer, she was pleased to know that her sister had so many people in her life who cared about her.

Glancing at the clock, she felt a niggle of unease as she tried to remember if she'd given Moira directions on how to prepare Cody's cereal. Maybe she could slip out to make a quick call…

The rest of the thought faded away when he walked through the door.

Wilder.

Her heart skipped a beat, then raced.

She'd wondered if he might show up. After all, he'd had a close and personal relationship with her sister—at least for a while. On the other hand, seventeen hundred miles seemed a long way to travel to say a final goodbye to a woman he hadn't seen in more than a year.

But maybe there was another reason he'd decided to make the trip. Maybe he did get the results of the DNA test and had confirmed that Cody was his child. And maybe, when he returned to Montana again, he intended to take his son with him.

That was something she definitely couldn't think about right now or she'd completely lose it.

"Hey," he said.

"Hi." She stood there awkwardly, not knowing whether to offer her hand or initiate a hug.

He made the decision for her, wrapping his arms around her and drawing her close. And during that all too brief moment, she felt such a sense of peace she wished she could stay in his arms forever.

But of course she couldn't. So she eased away and said, "It was nice of you to come all this way to pay your respects."

"I didn't come only for Leighton," he said. "I came for you, too."

His admission had her fighting against a fresh surge of emotion. "Why?"

"Because I didn't want you to be alone today."

Her eyes filled with tears then, but she refused to let them fall. "Thank you," she said, sincerely touched.

"How are you holding up?"

"I'm doing okay," she said.

"Of course, you are. Because who would keep everything together if you fell apart?" he mused.

"Believe me, I've had my moments."

She turned automatically to shake hands and exchange a few words with another visitor she didn't know, before shifting her attention back to Wilder.

"You got the test results," she guessed.

"Let's talk about that later," he suggested.

She nodded, because he was right—this wasn't the time or the place. And really, didn't she already know what the results were? The only question now was what Wilder intended to do, and that was definitely better left until later.

"Cody was here earlier," she said, certain he had to be wondering about the baby's whereabouts. "But I didn't think he needed to make the trip to the cemetery, so he's with my neighbor now. Plus, you know how cranky he gets if he misses a nap."

"Yeah." Wilder smiled. "I do know."

"But he's sleeping almost through the night now," she said.

"Are *you*?" he asked gently.

She just shook her head as the minister took his place at the podium. Wilder linked their hands and guided her to the front row, while the other mourners took seats around them.

She hadn't realized how much she dreaded having to

get through the service on her own until he was there and she was no longer alone.

Afterward, they rode together to the cemetery, then Wilder took her back to the funeral home where she'd left her vehicle.

"Do you want to come back to my place?" she asked, and immediately felt hot color rush into her cheeks. "I didn't mean that to sound like I was propositioning you."

"I didn't interpret it as a proposition," he said, then winked. "Unfortunately."

"I only meant that I'm sure you want to see Cody," she explained.

"I do," he confirmed. "But I'll come by in a couple hours, if that's okay. I've got a few things I need to do first."

"I'll see you in a couple hours then."

Beth had to buzz him into the building, so when the knock finally sounded on her door, she expected to find Wilder on the other side. Instead, she found Santa.

Though she couldn't have imagined anything would make her smile today, she felt her lips curve as she stood back to allow him entry. "You're a long way from the North Pole."

Her visitor responded with a hearty: "Ho! Ho! Ho!"

She lifted a brow. "And isn't Santa usually on holidays this time of year?"

"Usually," he agreed. "But Cody was out of town on Christmas Eve, so I had to take all his presents back to the North Pole with me. And then yesterday, Tracker—the elf who keeps track of all the good little girls and boys—told me that I could find Cody here."

"Tracker?" she echoed, amused by his elaborate narrative.

"Just go with it," he urged in a stage whisper.

"Well, Tracker was right," Beth confirmed. "Cody is here."

She led "Santa" to the living room, where the baby was propped up by a pillow on the floor, gnawing on the paw of the teddy bear that was one of the gifts she'd given to him at the Ambling A.

"Ho! Ho! Ho! Merry Christmas in January," Santa said.

Cody's eyes grew wide and wary as he looked at the stranger in the red suit, then his lower lip began to quiver.

"I should have reminded you that he slept through his visit with Saint Nick when I took him to the mall," Beth said. "So this is the first time he's actually seen Santa."

And if the terrified look in his eyes was any indication, Cody wasn't too impressed.

Sensing that a meltdown was imminent, Santa immediately pulled off his wig and beard, revealing his true identity to the little boy. "Hey, buddy."

Cody's lip stopped quivering and he offered a tentative smile, showing off his two teeth.

Wilder dropped his bag of presents onto the floor and picked up the baby. "I can't believe how much I missed this little guy," he confided to Beth.

"He missed you, too."

"How about you?" he asked. "Did you miss me?"

She was reluctant to answer the question. She didn't want to admit how very much she'd missed him, how much her heart ached whenever she thought about him—which was pretty much constantly. "Maybe," she said instead. "A little."

"Just a little, huh?" He sounded disappointed. "I missed you a lot from the moment you were gone—and then a little bit more each day."

She was surprised by his admission. "You did?"

He nodded. "As the youngest of six brothers raised by a single dad, I sometimes struggle to find the right words to express how I'm feeling," he confided to her now. "At other times, I struggle to even acknowledge that I have feelings.

"But I can't deny the way I feel about you any longer. I don't want to deny my feelings. I want a life with you, Beth. I want you and me and Cody to be together. A family."

It was what she wanted, too. More than anything. But she was afraid to trust that his feelings—and her own—were real. "We've only known each other a couple of weeks," she reminded him. "And our whole relationship, if it could even be called a relationship, revolved around Cody."

"Not our whole relationship," he said pointedly.

She knew he was referring to New Year's Eve—the night they'd enjoyed a very small and intimate celebration together—and she felt her cheeks flush with color. But as fabulous as that night had been, and as much as she might want to repeat it—over and over again—he was the one who'd told her that he didn't do relationships, that he wasn't capable of falling in love.

So this apparent turnaround was a little too sudden and abrupt to be believable. No matter how much she wanted to believe. Which led her to another, more logical conclusion. "I can appreciate that you're probably reeling from the DNA results," she said. "And now you're looking for someone to take care of your son, and I'm the obvious choice because—"

Wilder shook his head, cutting her off. "You have some serious insecurities, don't you?" he asked, seeming sincerely baffled by her speculation.

She shrugged. "Leighton was the beautiful one, the fun one," she said, though she doubted he needed the reminder. "I was always the other one."

"Leighton was beautiful and fun, and we had some good times together," he acknowledged. "But I was never in love with your sister."

She blinked, not sure she understood what he was saying.

"You, Lisbeth, are just as beautiful and just as much fun. You are also warm and kind, generous and loving, and I am head over heels in love with you."

For a long minute, she could only stare at him, stunned by his declaration. "You love me?"

"I love you, Lisbeth Ames," he confirmed.

"I didn't even think you *liked* me all that much."

He smiled. "I had some reservations at first, as I know you did about me, too."

She couldn't deny that was true.

"But over the past couple of weeks, everything changed. *You* changed everything for me," he told her. "And I can't imagine my life without you and Cody in it. Because, as it turns out, I've fallen head over heels for the little guy, too."

"I'm still waiting for you to confirm that you got the DNA results," she told him.

"I got them. And when I finally had the envelope in hand, I knew that whatever was written on the page didn't matter as much as what was in my heart." He looked at the baby in his arms. "And in my heart, Cody was already mine. The lab report only confirmed it."

She smiled then, her heart overflowing with happiness for her nephew and his daddy.

"You know, now would be a good time to tell me that you love me, too…if you do," Wilder said.

She lifted her gaze to his, so he would see in her eyes the truth that filled her heart. "I do love you, Wilder Crawford."

He kissed her then, long and slow and sweet.

And just when Beth had decided that she would be happy to go on kissing him forever, he eased his mouth from hers and said, "Now it's time for Cody's second first Christmas."

"Second first Christmas?" she asked, amused.

"Well, I didn't have any presents for him when you celebrated his first Christmas, so I brought these," he said, dumping the contents of the bag onto the floor.

She looked at the assortment of presents—small ones and big ones, hard ones and squishy ones—then at the man in the Santa suit. "Did you buy out The Toy Box?" she asked, referring to the local specialty store.

He grinned. "Not entirely."

"And you said I went overboard."

He shrugged, unrepentant. "I think I'm entitled to go a little overboard for my son's first Christmas."

"I think so, too," she agreed.

They both knelt on the floor to help Cody open his gifts. There were wooden puzzles and more books, a cuddly octopus learning toy, a ball that flashed colored lights, a miniature piano, a set of maracas, a drum, a xylophone and a tambourine.

"Are you trying to turn him into a one-baby band?" Beth teased.

"I read that there's a strong correlation between music and brain development," he explained.

"Was that in the book?" she asked, echoing the same question he'd once asked her.

"There isn't one book that's the authority on everything," he said, echoing her response. "And every baby is different."

"But most parents would probably agree that they're more interested in boxes and bows than presents at this age," she said, noting how intently Cody was focused on the shiny green bow in his hand.

"There's one more," Wilder said, setting the last small square box on the floor in front of her. "For you."

"For me?" Her heart pounded inside her chest as she tore off the paper to reveal a velvet jeweler's box. With unsteady hands, she opened the lid to reveal a dazzling diamond solitaire.

She lifted her stunned gaze from the ring to find Wilder watching her. His expression was intent, serious—and just a little bit uncertain.

He cleared his throat. "Maybe it's too soon," he allowed. "But—"

"No," she quickly interjected, shaking her head.

"No?" he echoed.

His bleak tone and grim expression immediately alerted her to his misinterpretation of her response.

"No, it's not too soon," she hastened to clarify. "But you can't just hand a woman a ring—you have to ask the question."

"Oh." He released an audible sigh of relief. "Okay, I can do that," he said. "Beth Ames, will you—"

"Yes," she said, interjecting again.

He chuckled softly and slid the ring on her finger. "A perfect fit—just like you and me and Cody."

Epilogue

Five months later

"I now pronounce you husband and wife." The minister nodded to the groom. "You may kiss your bride."

Wilder didn't need to be told twice. He lowered his head and touched his mouth to Beth's, lingering for just a moment—sealing their vows, promising his heart.

Then they turned to face their guests, and the bride lifted her skirt just enough to show off the cowboy boots she'd donned beneath her wedding gown. There were chuckles mixed in with the applause then, and the happy couple joined hands to exit along the aisle of their makeshift outdoor chapel—pausing first at the front row of chairs so the groom could take his now ten-month-old son from the boy's grandfather.

As Beth and Wilder mingled with their guests, she couldn't help but reflect on how much had changed in her life in just six months. And although she still missed her sister every day, she took comfort in knowing that Leighton lived on in her little boy, who demonstrated more and more each day that he had his mother's happy disposition and his father's effortless charm.

Those traits had been on full display as he enchanted the guests who'd come to the Ambling A for the wedding of his biological father to his maternal aunt. And there were a lot of guests. In addition to Wilder's immediate family and all the distant Rust Creek Falls Crawford relatives, there were Daltons, Traubs, Stocktons, Joneses and O'Reillys. Beth had heard more names today than she could ever be expected to remember, but she was happy to be starting a life and raising Cody in this close-knit community—even if it meant a wedding reception far bigger than she'd ever anticipated.

Thankfully the whole day had been planned with meticulous attention to detail by Vivienne Dalton, who continued to circulate to ensure that everything went according to plan. Her only failing was an inability to corral Hunter's seven-year-old daughter. Wren kept returning to the chapel to practice walking down the aisle and tossing flower petals, in preparation for her very important role as flower girl when her daddy finally married Merry in only a few more weeks.

After a delicious meal—interrupted by countless toasts to the happy couple—the bride and groom shared their first dance. As the song drew to a close, the rest of the guests were invited to join them, and Beth was pleased to see each of Wilder's brothers on the floor with their partners. Even Finn and Avery were dancing, having enlisted Max to keep an eye on their beautiful three-month-old daughter, Mabel.

Of course, the proud grandpa was happy to have his arms full of babies. And Wren, finally satisfied that she'd had sufficient practice being a flower girl, was helping mind her younger cousins.

When the bride and groom took a reprieve from dancing and returned to their table with Cody, Beth found an obviously old but beautiful jewel-encrusted book beside her bouquet.

"What's this?" she asked, as Cody reached out to touch the sparkly stones on the cover.

"My brothers believe it's Josiah Abernathy's diary," Wilder said, and proceeded to give her a brief history of the book and the writer's forbidden love affair with a mysterious woman.

"But why is it here?" she wondered.

"They've been passing it around for months, claiming it carries a love spell or something like that. I guess they've decided it's our turn to experience its powers."

"All true," Merry confirmed, as she joined them. "But there's more—a note hidden inside the cover confirmed the mystery writer as Josiah Abernathy and his girlfriend as Winona Cobbs.

"Even more shocking," she continued, as the rest of Wilder's siblings and their spouses gathered around, "is that their baby girl wasn't stillborn, as she believed. Beatrix was taken away and given to another family to raise."

A revelation that led to much speculation about whether it might be possible to find Beatrix after so much time had passed.

"This is all very fascinating," Wilder said, speaking quietly so that only his bride could hear him. "But what I really want to know is when we can steal away from this party."

"You're not having a good time?" she asked, surprised.

"The wedding was great," he acknowledged. "But now, Mrs. Crawford, I'm more than ready to start the honeymoon."

She tipped her head back to smile at him. "I like the sound of that, Mr. Crawford."

As if on cue, their wedding planner stepped up beside them to ask, "What are you still doing here when the honeymoon suite at Maverick Manor is waiting for you?"

"We're on our way," Wilder said. "We just wanted to thank you for giving us the perfect day."

"Well, I did have a little help from Mother Nature," Vivienne said, gesturing to the sun setting against a cloudless sky. "But I'm happy to take credit for all the rest."

"If only you'd had as much success as a matchmaker," Logan said to her.

"I think I did pretty well helping you and your brothers find your perfect matches."

"What are you talking about?" Xander asked. "We found our own matches."

Vivienne smiled. "Did you?"

The brothers exchanged puzzled glances.

"I might not have introduced Logan and Sarah, but they met at my office," she pointed out. "And Xander and Lily only got together because I'd set up a date between Knox and Lily, then Knox rushed to marry Genevieve because he didn't want any part of Max's scheme. I also knew Finn and Avery would be perfect together, even if I didn't know they'd already found one another, and it was because they were getting married that Hunter decided to hire a nanny and fell in love with Merry."

Wilder nodded his agreement. "It looks like you did have a hand in five out of six matches," he said to Vivienne.

"I might have found someone for you, too," she told him. "Except that you managed to find your perfect match without any help."

"Actually, *I* found *him*," Beth said, making her husband smile.

"Five out of six is an impressive stat," Finn acknowledged. "But still short of Max's target."

"And nothing less than one hundred percent is ever good enough for Maximilian Crawford," Knox remarked.

"I think I could make a case for six out of seven," the wedding planner–slash–matchmaker said, nodding toward the dance floor where the groom's father was slow dancing with the woman Wilder recognized from New Year's Eve.

"Who's that?" Beth asked, because she hadn't been at the party at Maverick Manor.

"Estelle, my former boss," Vivienne told them.

"I thought she moved to Phoenix," Lily remarked.

"And then she came back. She said she enjoyed the

more temperate climate, but planning funerals was as depressing as hell."

"Dad seems completely smitten with her," Logan remarked, apparently baffled that such a tiny woman could have captivated the larger-than-life cattleman.

"She's got a personality equal to his own," Vivienne assured him. "And Max is so happy with the way things worked out for everyone that he's agreed to honor the terms of our original contract. As a result, we'll be able to fix the roof at Sawmill Station *and* invest more money in the Thunder Canyon operation. Plus, with the way business is booming, I'm thinking of hiring extra help in Rust Creek Falls, too."

"What kind of experience is needed to work in the wedding planning business?" Beth wondered, her curiosity piqued.

"Are you looking for a job?" Vivienne asked hopefully.

"I am," the bride confirmed. "And there are no teaching positions currently available at the local elementary school."

"Do you believe in happy endings?"

Beth looked up at her new husband, and the love that filled her heart to overflowing shone through her eyes. "I do now."

Vivienne smiled. "That's a good start."

Cody apparently thought so, too, because he clapped his hands together.

Wilder's chuckle drew the little boy's attention to him. Then Cody reached his arms up toward his daddy and said his first word: "Da-da."

And Beth thought that was the perfect ending to a perfect day—and a very happy beginning for the start of their life together as a family.

* * * * *

Catch up with the rest of the
Montana Mavericks: Six Brides for Six Brothers

Look for:
Her Favorite Maverick
by New York Times *bestselling author*
Christine Rimmer

Rust Creek Falls Cinderella
by Melissa Senate

The Maverick's Wedding Wager
by Joanna Sims

The Maverick's Secret Baby
by Teri Wilson

Maverick Holiday Magic
by Teresa Southwick

Maverick Christmas Surprise
by Brenda Harlen

Available now wherever Harlequin books
and ebooks are sold.

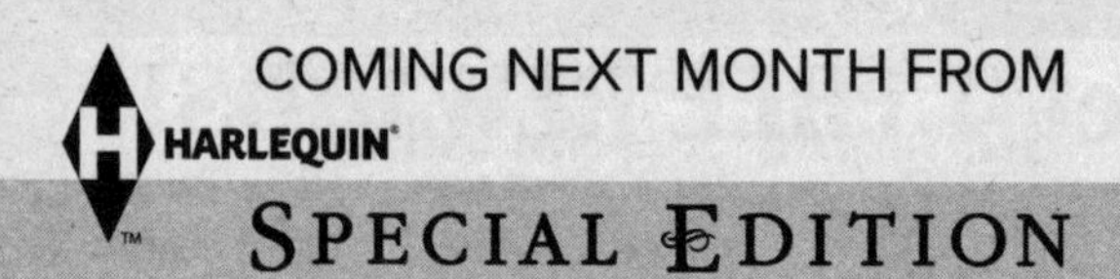

Available December 17, 2019

#2737 FORTUNE'S FRESH START

The Fortunes of Texas: Rambling Rose • by Michelle Major

In the small Texas burg of Rambling Rose, real estate investor Callum Fortune is making a big splash. The last thing he needs is any personal complications slowing his pace—least of all nurse Becky Averill, a beautiful widow with twin baby girls!

#2738 HER RIGHT-HAND COWBOY

Forever, Texas • by Marie Ferrarella

A clause in her father's will requires Ena O'Rourke to work the family ranch for six months before she can sell it. She's livid at her father throwing a wrench in her life from beyond the grave. But Mitch Randall, foreman of the Double E, is always there for her. As Ena spends more time on the ranch—and with Mitch—new memories are laid over the old...and perhaps new opportunities to make a life.

#2739 SECOND-CHANCE SWEET SHOP

Wickham Falls Weddings • by Rochelle Alers

Brand-new bakery owner Sasha Manning didn't anticipate that the teenager she hired would have a father more delectable than anything in her shop window! Sasha still smarts from falling for a man too good to be true. Divorced single dad Dwight Adams will have to prove to Sasha that he's the real deal and not a wolf in sheep's clothing...and learn to trust someone with his heart along the way.

#2740 COOKING UP ROMANCE

The Taylor Triplets • by Lynne Marshall

Lacy was a redhead with a pink food truck who prepared mouthwatering meals. Hunky construction manager Zack Gardner agreed to let her feed his hungry crew in exchange for cooking lessons for his young daughter. But it looked like the lovely businesswoman was transforming the single dad's life in more ways than one—since a family secret is going to change both of their lives in ways they never expected.

#2741 RELUCTANT HOMETOWN HERO

Wildfire Ridge • by Heatherly Bell

Former army officer Ryan Davis doesn't relish the high-profile role of town sheriff, but when duty calls, he responds. Even if it means helping animal rescuer Zoey Castillo find her missing foster dog. When Ryan asks her out, Zoey is wary of a relationship in the spotlight—especially given her past. If the sheriff wants to date her, he'll have to prove that two legs are better than four.

#2742 THE WEDDING TRUCE

Something True • by Kerri Carpenter

For the sake of their best friends' wedding, divorce attorney Xander Ryan and wedding planner Grace Harris are calling a truce. Now they must plan the perfect wedding shower together. But Xander doesn't believe in marriage! And Grace believes in romance and true love. Clearly, they have nothing in common. In fact, all Xander feels when Grace is near is disdain and...desire. Wait. What?

YOU CAN FIND MORE INFORMATION ON UPCOMING HARLEQUIN® TITLES, FREE EXCERPTS AND MORE AT WWW.HARLEQUIN.COM.

HSECNM1219